Half My Blood

A Dartmoor Novella

Lauren Gilley

The Dartmoor Series

Fearless

Price of Angels

Half My Blood

The Skeleton King (coming soon)

Half My Blood

HALF MY BLOOD
ISBN-13: 978-1514212325
ISBN-10: 1514212323
ASIN: B00XPUSUUO

HP Press
Atlanta, GA

Dear Reader,

This book wasn't part of the plan. It wasn't even supposed to be a book; it began as a very short story. But it had a mind of its own, as do all stories, because Holly, and Michael, and Ava, and Mercy, and Aidan, and Tango had some things to tell you before the series continues. Some of them wanted to tie up loose threads; and some of them wanted to unravel a few. They want you to know that this is not a standalone adventure, if an adventure it can even be called. What you are about to read is a slice of life, told in the literary way I know how to tell things, skipping across the Dartmoor landscape without regard for genre or propriety.

This one's for the fans. For the readers who want more. It is a "thank you" for supporting this plucky little book series. I hope you enjoy it.

Happy Reading, always.

~Lauren

Half My Blood

~*~

Blood has been one of the primary flavors of my life. It isn't now. Now, it's been over a year since it flowed across my tongue, all salt and heat, dark copper chocolate. You don't grow up at the mercy of a man's fists without knowing well the taste of your own blood, welling up from the splits in your cheeks, and tongue, and broken lips. The taste was never what frightened me – it was the sight of it. The way it shines in the sun when it's wet, glassy on top. It stops my heart every time – looking at spilled blood.

Usually.

But last week, I found a place at the top of a page in Moby Dick, a little dark stain where the paper had cut Michael's finger. Not my blood. Not Mama's spilled in dark rancid stains on the rumpled sheets. Not Abraham's in the snow. Dewey's on the blade of the knife. Jacob's steaming on Cassius's muzzle. I can still hear the dog ripping into them sometimes, if I close my eyes and think about snow.

But this was Michael's blood, and it had spilled on accident, and it was just a little spot.

My husband's blood.

The blood that makes up half of the little girl in my belly.

My girl...

Holly McCall

Half My Blood

One
The Henley Street Bridge

For Aidan, it wasn't the University of Tennessee's sprawling brick campus, but the Henley Street Bridge that stood as signature monument in his hometown of Knoxville. His father's empire crouched on the banks of the Tennessee River, and if he stood at the shore, the brackish smell of water filling his lungs, he could look upriver and see the bridge, its soaring arches black silhouettes against the ragged orange of the sunset. It had never been the posh university scene to which he'd belonged, but to the industrial, dirty-handed river side of the city. In a way, it felt like he'd grown up in the shadow of that bridge. His ancestors hadn't been the ones to build the school – they'd built the concrete and steel miracle of infrastructure instead.

He had no illusions about his bloodline.

He didn't kid himself about the picture he presented to the citizens of Knoxville. He knew what they thought of him; no golden boy, him, no. A little wicked curiosity from the young women, censure and fear from the old. Men both admired and hated him on sight. No matter what Hollywood pretended, outlaws would never be in style. It was impossible to be popular when your arms were orange and blue and red and black with ink.

It was early evening as he hit the bridge, a molten sunset sliding over the city, flaring in car windows and glinting off street signs.

Behind his shades, Aidan surveyed the opposite bank, and grinned to himself as he gunned the throttle and shot across the river. His Harley always sounded a little different when he was on the Henley Street Bridge, a strange echoing with all that space between the biker and the water, separated only by the asphalt under the tires.

The water was jewel-toned in the fading light. The breeze was strong against his face, whistling over his ears, pressing little lines into his skin – aging him, just as it had aged all his brothers.

It was wonderful.

Too soon, he was clear of the bridge and heading into the bustling heart of the city. He had nowhere to be; he was just cruising. Coming back from an errand Ghost had sent him on – "Go see what Fish is up to" – and one that was clearly just busy-work at that, he felt no rush to be back at the shop. Merc was there; Merc was the best mechanic they had, and didn't need overseeing. Aidan planned on getting back in time so he could let his brother-in-law knock off early, go home, have dinner with Ava and the baby. And he, single to his bones, would work OT, pick up some extra change, have just enough dough to buy half-decent wine to try and bribe Jenny Newsom into a date. And by date, he meant hooking up on her sofa.

He had no place to be, and was enjoying the wind in his face, and the sights and smells of his city.

It *was* his city, wasn't it?

People would have argued with him; said Knoxville belonged to the Vols, to its law-abiding citizens. But like any marriage, could a man claim ownership if he hadn't seen and embraced the dark parts? He didn't know; he'd have to ask one of his married brothers about that. Not Mercy, though, because his sister was just his sister, and didn't count among his notions of married women. Regardless, he felt at least a part-owner of Knoxville. And he loved this city.

It was with regret that he coasted to a halt at the next red light.

At first.

In the left-hand lane alongside him sat a putrid yellow Mustang convertible. He mentally berated the driver for both the color and his choice of a drop-top; hideously uncool. Nearest him, in the passenger seat, a girl shook out her windblown blonde hair and turned to him with obvious interest, a dazzling smile splitting her suntanned face.

Aidan smirked. It never failed; the ladies loved the bike.

As he watched her, the blonde leaned over the door of the Mustang, giving him a view down her shirt; she was squeezing her breasts together for effect.

"I like your bike!" she called over the grumble of car and Harley, grinning again.

He grinned back. "You wanna ride?"

She laughed and sat back, tossing her hair. "I dunno…" She gestured to the driver next to her.

The guy was dark-haired, and looked like he lived in a gym. Tight t-shirt and Oakley shades. Typical prick.

Aidan gave a dismissive snort she probably couldn't hear. "Fuck him," he said. "He's got a goddamn *yellow* car."

He couldn't hear her laughter, but could see it in her wide smile and convulsing shoulders.

And then her boyfriend noticed what was going on, and shot Aidan an ugly scowl across the car. He said something to the girl Aidan couldn't hear, and the girl tossed her hair and shot him back a dirty look of her own.

Aidan couldn't wipe the smirk off his face.

The boyfriend glared at him again, and then came the most universal invitation known to competitive mankind. He revved his engine.

It didn't sound bad – clearly, he had a V8 under the hood on his yellow travesty of a muscle car. But all the major US automakers had long since leashed their muscular beasts, and it wasn't the indomitable throaty growl of Mustangs long past. It sure as hell couldn't compete with the sound of Aidan's pipes as he answered the revving with one of his own.

Cross-traffic was slackening in the intersection in front of them. The light was getting ready to change.

The douche in the car gave Aidan a level stare over the top of his girlfriend's head. The blonde turned and folded her arms over the ledge of the open window, openly watching Aidan, grinning like mad.

Aidan had no doubt that if he whooped this guy's ass bad enough, that girl would be on the back of his bike in a heartbeat.

He sent his competitor a challenging grin. His hands tensed, fingers twitching inside his leather gloves. The soles of his feet tingled in anticipation.

The cars were stopping at the balk line.

Green light coming in *five*…

He cranked the throttle.

…*four*…

The Mustang growled in answer.

…*three*…

The Harley's rear tire screamed; Aidan could smell the acrid stink of burning rubber, and knew he was kicking up a vaporous cloud of smoke.

…*two*…

"Eat shit, dickhead," Aidan called, and the blonde's mouth opened in silent laughter, painted lips stretched wide over white teeth.

…*one.*

The thing civilians didn't understand about a Harley Dyna Super Glide is that it was *fast.* They always expected to get whipped by crotch rockets, but they never counted on the sinister black Harley showing them up.

Aidan got the jump on the Mustang, thanks to lightness alone, and then his engine put the leashed fuel-efficient V8 to shame. If it was Holly McCall's Chevelle SS he was running against, he might have had a problem, but not now. Now, he flew off the balk line and laughed as the Mustang surged along his flank, trying to catch him.

He and Tango had raced at this light before, from it to the next one, and it was a little over a quarter mile, and arrow-straight. He knew this stretch of Knoxville road like he knew the tattoos running up both arms; he could have run this race with his eyes shut. And so he risked a glance back over his shoulder, to see the blonde's hair whipping around her head, to see the driver glaring at him, lips moving as he muttered curses. Aidan grinned at them, and thought he saw the blonde wave at him.

Then he faced the road again…

Just in time to see a tow-headed little boy dart off the sidewalk and into his path.

The world stopped.

It simply ceased to exist.

His friends, his family, his club. His bike and his tats and his favorite gloves curled tight around the grips, the flaring chrome of his handlebars. The beers he wanted to drink, the pool he wanted to shoot, the girls he wanted to bed. The things he wanted to prove to his father. All of it gone, in that instant. He wasn't Aidan Teague – the biker, the Lean Dog, the son, the stepson, the half-brother, the club-brother – but a weapon bearing down on the oblivious child chasing his dropped toy out into the street.

In the vacuum, in those few seconds when he lost all touch with himself, Aidan noticed so many details. The woman on the sidewalk, obviously the boy's mother, lurching after the boy, face contorted in a horrified scream. The faces turned toward him on the other side of the coffee shop window, their features blurred by glaring sunlight. The pale whitish streaks in the boy's hair; hair pretty enough to belong to a girl, styled in an unfortunate bowl cut. The grit and glass-glimmer of the pavement. The sweat trickling down his temples, his head too hot beneath his helmet.

A photographic moment, one that seemed to last hours, rather than seconds.

I'm going to kill him, Aidan realized.

The boy turned his head, and the sunlight fell on his soft-featured face, eyes glinting like blue marbles as they opened wide at the sight of the bike bearing down on him.

No, Aidan thought. *I'm not.* And he lurched heavily to the left, swerving into the other lane. The Mustang's lane, he remembered, the same moment something clipped the back of his bike and a shudder went through the machine.

The last thing he saw, before the blackness closed in, was the bright blue dome of the sky overhead, arching over the building roofs, pouring sun down into his eyes. It was beautiful. It felt like he was flying.

And then nothing.

Two
A House is Not a Home

One Week Earlier

"Ooh, those go in the kitchen," Ava said as she spied the rum box containing her new yellow dinner dishes come through the open front door in Tango's arms. "You can set them on the table. Careful; they're breakable." They'd also cost her three weeks' worth of income working part time helping her mom out at the Dartmoor office.

Tango nodded, but paused beside her, sunlight sparking off all his earrings, glimmering in his light hair. He nodded toward the sleeping lump of baby in her arms. "He can sleep through all this?"

Remy's breath was warm, wet, and steady in the middle of her breastbone, where she had him tucked against her chest, both arms cradling him. "Like his daddy. Dead to the world."

He grinned. "That's a big baby." It wasn't the first time he'd said that to her.

She smiled. "I was sort of there when he came into the world. Yeah, he's big."

With a delicate *ouch* face he moved on, heading for the kitchen with the plates.

Aidan came tromping in next, dry caked mud falling from his boot treads onto the hardwood, a rolled-up rug slung over one shoulder. He and Tango were both down to their white wifebeaters, and those were plastered to them with sweat.

"You just had to move on a day that was hot as balls, didn't you?"

Ava smiled sweetly at her brother. "It's the middle of July, bro. When do you think it's going to stop being hot as balls?"

"Dunno. But that woulda been the time to move."

"Right. I elect you as the one to tell Mercy he should've held off on buying the house."

He made a complicated face that she wanted to laugh at. "Yeah..." He and Mercy may have been almost as close as real brothers, but Merc had drawn a line when it came to his tiny personal family. Aidan knew not to step over it too far. "Where does this go?" He hefted the rug higher on his shoulder.

"Living room, in front of the sofa."

14

Which wasn't much of a walk, because the narrow foyer led into said living room.

"Right." Aidan headed that way, the ornate tangle of thorns and red roses clustered at the tops of his shoulders shining as the sunlight struck the fine sheen of sweat on his skin. The tats were detailed, richly colored, and expansive, his largest – trailing all the way down his triceps on both sides, a few stray petals and thorns along his ribs, under his arms. Of all his ink, those tattoos were Ava's favorites. His mantle of roses.

The incoming biker moving crew kept coming. Carter and Harry toted the dressing table between them, and Ava gave them directions. As prospects, they weren't allowed to gripe about the heat and the work, but Carter gave her a wink as he said, "Yes, ma'am," and managed a half-mocking courtly bow as he passed.

"I think you need a new sponsor," she told him, "my brother's going to ruin you."

Carter laughed, and he and Harry's shuffled footfalls moved around the corner.

Littlejohn had coffee mugs and silverware, and she steered him toward the kitchen.

Maggie walked in next, casually glamorous in loose white shirt, Bermuda shorts, heels and high ponytail, her sunglasses pushed up on her head. She held two tall paper cups from Stella's Café, and handed one to Ava. "Sweet tea."

"Stella makes the best." Ava shifted Remy into a one-armed hold, clasping him to her chest, and took the tea with the other.

Maggie surveyed the progress around them. "How's it going?"

Ava smiled wryly. "Considerably less has happened since you left."

Maggie *tsk*ed. "You've got a ways to grow into your bossiness. You've got to assert yourself more, baby, until they get in the habit of listening better."

She hid another smile in her cup as she sipped tea, secretly sure that she'd never pull off her mother's airy command of all things masculine in Lean Dog Land.

"Don't fuss at them, though. They *are* being good help."

"Hmm," Maggie agreed.

As if they'd sensed the arrival of lunch, all the movers appeared together in the living room.

"Food's out on the picnic table," Maggie said, jerking her head toward the door.

"Thank Christ," Aidan muttered.

Maggie swatted the flat of his belly as he passed. "You're not quite to the starvation point yet. I got back just in time, huh?"

"Um, yeah."

Tango, ever graceful, said, "Thanks for picking it up," and paused to reach for his wallet, intending to pay for his takeout.

Maggie shook her head. "Absolutely not. You *are* at the starvation point," she said affectionately. "Go eat."

Tango blushed, ducked his head, and said, "Thanks, Mags," on his way out.

When the boys were all outside, converging on the picnic table in the driveway like hyenas on a wildebeest carcass, Maggie said, "You wanna walk around and see where we stand?"

She meant organization- and design-wise, and Ava would be glad for the input. She nodded. "Yeah."

It was a small house. An old house, one with creaky hardwood floors and badly outdated windows, air streaming in around the edges of the panes with a faint whistle when she put her ear close enough to listen. It was framed with white wood siding, and boasted a brick chimney, and a narrow front porch just large enough for a single rocking chair and side table. It had a detached garage, and a covered walkway that led to the side door off the mud room. The kitchens and bathrooms were original, similar to the kitchen and bathroom they'd left behind at the apartment above the bakery in town.

And it was their house, hers and Mercy's. And little Remy's.

Two weeks before, Mercy had come home from work buzzing with energy, as jittery as a kid on Christmas morning. He'd had a real estate flier in his hand, the kind of pamphlet they put in the information boxes up at the street with For Sale signs. "I talked to the agent," he'd said, without even pausing long enough to kiss her hello. "And she said there's other people interested, and we'd have to move fast if we wanted it."

"Wanted what?" she'd asked, bewildered.

"This house!" He'd shoved the flier at her, breathing through his mouth like he'd run a race.

They'd gone first thing the next morning to look at it, arriving early before the agent could let them in, walking through the backyard and peering through the windows, hands cupped around their eyes against the glare of the sun as they pressed inquisitive faces to the glass.

Not a big house, no, but much bigger than the apartment – three bedrooms, two full baths, a decent yard, two-car garage, and a basement with enough floor space and high enough ceilings that Mercy could finish it out, if they wanted, should the need arise. Say…if they had all five of the children he had only half-joked about siring.

The place needed some TLC, but didn't everything? Didn't giant Cajun biker poets need some good loving in order to turn into responsible, house-buying husbands? Yes, and yes.

Ava had been plagued with reservations, mainly because of their lackluster finances. But also because leaving the apartment put an awful lump in her throat.

Mercy had confessed that, barring rent and a biker part here and there, he'd been exceptionally thrifty for years. And so with only a little loan from Dartmoor, and the bank's grudging approval, they'd become homeowners. Felix Louis and Ava Rose Lécuyer, sign where the arrows indicate, please.

And now it was moving day.

"You've got good light in here," Maggie said as they stepped into the master bedroom.

It was at the end of the hall, decently separate from the two spare bedrooms, and it had windows on three sides, pouring in hazy summer sunlight.

"The bed can go under that window," Maggie said, indicating the center of the far wall. "And your dresser there."

Ava nodded and adjusted Remy so her arms were more comfortable. He was a heavy little bundle. "Yeah, that'll work."

Maggie turned to face her, her smile warm and knowing. "It's a lot, isn't it?"

A lot to think about, a lot to organize, a lot of change. Yeah – a lot.

"It is," she said with a sigh. "I realized, two nights ago when I was packing boxes, that I've never moved before. Not like this."

"It's hell. When your dad I moved out of his apartment, after you were born – Jesus, you never saw such a disaster. We had to be out by midnight, and we were cutting it too close. On the last trip, the car was so stuffed that your dad filled your carseat with a stack of t-shirts and let Aidan *hold you* while he rode shotgun."

Ava felt her brows leap up her forehead.

"When they pulled up to the house," Maggie said, shaking her head and smiling at the memory, "and I saw you in Aidan's lap, I almost had a full-on coronary standing in the driveway. My nerves were shot at that point, and I screamed at Kenny so bad, the neighbors stuck their heads out the window and asked if everything was alright. If there was ever a way to make a terrible first impression on the non-outlaws…"

"Can you imagine Dad doing something like that now?" Ava asked, a slow grin spreading across her face. "Captain Caution."

"He's a better daddy than he used to be," Maggie said. Then she reached her hands out in an unmistakable gesture. "Here, pass the hot potato. You look like your arms are getting tired."

Grateful for the break, Ava eased the sleeping baby over into her mother's arms and then wiggled her hands, willing the soreness from her tendons. A part of her regretted the loss of the small heartbeat against her breasts, the regular damp breaths on her skin. Every day of motherhood was a struggle between rationality and the powerful need to keep her baby wrapped safely in her arms.

Maggie tucked Remy up on her shoulder, a hand cradling the perfect round shape of his skull. Her expression became the thoughtful, X-ray assessing one that missed nothing. "You miss the old place, don't you?"

Ava glanced through the naked window, out at the overgrown gardenia bushes and their profusion of star-shaped blooms. "Yeah," she admitted. "It was special, you know? It was *him* for me."

Maggie was quiet a moment, then: "Maybe it's good to start fresh, then. This place can be *both* of you."

Ava sent her mother a small, thankful smile. "Yeah," she said, and the word echoed in the small hollow, aching part of her that didn't like letting go of the past.

There was a loud clomp of boots somewhere else in the house. Aidan called to them: "Where you'd guys go? Merc just got back with the refrigerator."

Ava hitched up her shoulders and drew in a deep breath. "Back to work, then."

"Uncle Wynn?" Holly called, pausing at the entrance of the barn. The smells of hay and warm animals and the pleasant tang of barn dust welcomed her, pungent in the summer heat.

There was an answering bray from one of the donkeys.

And then Wynn called, "Back here, darlin'!"

She knew the inside of the barn well at this point, and she navigated the slightly meandering aisle flanked by irregular stalls with familiarity. The overhead lights were off at this time of day, and sunlight streamed in dusty shafts through the open windows. All the animals were outside, save one. Wynn waited for her outside a large box stall, leaning on the door.

He glanced up at her approach, smile splitting his broad face. "You're just in time; he's just wakin' up from his nap."

"Oh, good." Holly felt a flutter of true excitement in the pit of her ever-expanding stomach.

Michael's uncle Wynford was a big man, tall and big-boned, with great careful paws for hands, and a square jaw gone soft with age. He looked nothing like his nephew, and instead looked more like the brawny, working-man types Holly had known growing up. Known...and dreaded. But Wynn had proved himself immediately as kind, respectful, and gentle. A storybook farmer, at times. The first time Holly slipped and called him uncle, he'd smiled and invited her to keep doing it.

He smelled like hay and cow hide and damp dog hair as Holly sidled up beside him at the door of the large box stall.

Inside, Daisy the Jersey cow stood watching her two-day-old calf surge awkwardly to his feet, staggering on stick-legs, the fat knobs of knee and hock incongruous in the slender limbs as he got his balance. Daisy had been bred to a neighbor's Angus bull, and so the calf looked very much like one, coal black and nicely formed.

"My God," Holly breathed, breath catching. She clenched her hands on the top of the stall door, not minding the prick of splinters. "He's adorable!" She'd had the same reaction to little Remy Lécuyer, heart stuttering at the up-close sight of something so small and fragile and beautiful.

"He's been nursing real good," Wynn said of the calf. "And runnin' around in the stall. I'm gonna walk 'em out to the paddock. You wanna watch?"

"I can help," she offered.

"Nah, nah, you just stand off to the side." He waved toward the opposite side of the aisle. "Don't want you gettin' trampled now, do we? Michael'd have my hide if something happened to you or the baby."

A true statement.

Feeling unwieldy and useless, Holly stepped clear and watched from a safe distance as Wynn hooked a line to the sweet cow's halter and opened the stall door. Daisy plodded out after her master, the calf leaping to keep up.

There was a small, half-acre paddock that ran alongside the barn and that was where Wynn took Daisy and the baby. When he unclipped the lead, Daisy threw her face down into the thick summer grass and began grazing with gusto. The calf flicked his big ears, switched his tail, and surveyed this new domain with outward nervousness, glued to his mother's side.

"It's a shock, I guess," Wynn said as he latched the gate and came to stand beside Holly at the fence. "To go from in there to out here."

"I'd think so," Holly said, gaze on the little Angus as he sniffed experimentally at the grass.

"It's gotta be kinda what it's like for a real baby, you know?" he continued. "It's all warm and dark where they are, and then they're out in the bright big scary place." He shrugged. "Then again, I don't know that for sure. I don't remember bein' a baby and I never had one."

Something in his tone struck her. He'd been thrilled from the first when she and Michael had told him they were expecting. "Do you wish you'd had kids?" she asked, gently.

He made a face, sun striking harshly against the lines in his cheeks. "I dunno. Maybe, sometimes. I know I wouldn't have been any good at it, so it's just as well, I guess."

"That's not true," Holly scolded. "You would have been wonderful. You raised Michael." And in her book, men didn't turn out much better than Michael McCall.

The old man laughed. "That boy coulda raised himself. I was just there to get high things off the shelf."

Holly smiled.

"I'm just glad I'll get to be a great-uncle," Wynn said, turning to face her. "That's almost like being a grandpa, isn't it?"

She nodded. "I think so."

"Have you picked out a name yet?"

There went that stone again, sinking through her gut, a lot like dread, heavy on top of her womb. They'd just found out that it was a girl. Not an *it* – a *she*. But as far as names went, she hadn't the faintest idea. The more real motherhood began to seem, the more it terrified her.

"No," she said, letting her gaze drift off toward the clump of sweet gum trees at the edge of the paddock. "I haven't put much thought into it."

"Oh my God." Ava let herself go limp and fell backward across the bed. The double bed, not truly big enough for the two of them when one of them was six-foot-five, was the only thing "right" in the house. Before she'd left for the night, Maggie had instructed the boys in

20

reassembling the wood frame and situating box spring and mattress. She'd snapped on fresh sheets, put cases on the pillows, and done it up invitingly, covers turned down and ready for them.

Mercy, already flat on his back beside her, naked save for frayed plaid boxers, his clothes a heap on the floor beside the bed, stared up at the ceiling and said, "I need a shower. But I just don't care anymore."

" 'S'okay," Ava said. "We can be smelly and dirty together."

She'd fared a little better than Merc, though, having at least arranged her dirty clothes in a stack by the door, and pulled on one of his old t-shirts to sleep in. It smelled like the flowers of their detergent and his shampoo, while her skin smelled of sweat and work and exhaustion.

As a couple, they didn't own much, but lots of hand-me-down furniture donations had seen their way into the moving truck. In just the one day, they'd moved all their meager belongings – most of them books – and acquired a secondhand fridge, microwave, washer and dryer, since all the appliances at the apartment had had to stay, by mandate of the landlord.

The entire club had shown up, in shifts, to help with the move. Walsh had brought two chilled bottles of decent champagne; Ava had only had two sips, because she was breastfeeding, but the others had toasted the hell out of the new house. Walsh had given her a deft wink and said, "We'll celebrate for you, love," and taken a swig straight out of the bottle before passing it on to Mercy.

Michael had helped Mercy wedge the new dryer into its place in the narrow laundry closet alongside the guest bathroom. Since Ava had told Holly she was in no way to lift or tote anything in her condition, Michael had brought Holly's contribution -- a prepared lasagna ready to slide into the oven when they got hungry, along with rolls and chopped salad – and promised in his shy, awkward, stern way that his wife would come by tomorrow to help with organizing, along with Ava's friends. When Michael had held back from the end-of-the-night celebrating, Mercy had shoved a champagne bottle at him and said, "Crack a smile, man," with a broad, good-humored one of his own. Poor Michael was being sucked into a friendship with Mercy whether he wanted it or not. Judging by the quiet gleam in his eyes when no one was looking, Ava thought he wanted it.

The place was a shambles of boxes, and there was so much left to do, but finally, they were alone, and sleep was like a lead blanket hovering over them, ready to fall.

"Where's the little gator bait?" Mercy asked, voice dreamy with exhaustion.

"Sleeping." Ava rolled onto her side, so she could see her husband's noble Frenchman profile, so striking with his Cherokee coloring. "I put him down in the crib next door" – the room that would be his nursery – "so we could eat, and he's still out cold. So I left him." She felt a sudden spasm of maternal emotion. He'd been sleeping in their tiny bedroom at the apartment in his bassinet. She was used to falling asleep to the light patter of his breathing.

Mercy's head rolled toward her. "Does that mean we're alone?"

"It does. But I'm so tired – you get on if you want, but I can't promise I'll be real exciting right now."

He chuckled; the way his chest lifted, burnished in the lamplight, made her want to rethink that "tired" part. "Even I'm not that cruel, *fillette*. I'd just embarrass myself anyway." He reached to stroke her cheek with the back of his hand and she closed her eyes, sighing with contentment.

She loved when he was inside her, but loved when he was beside her, too. Like now, that undemanding love that was steeped in so many years of friendship and love and understanding.

"What's wrong?" he asked, as he studied her face, and she was reminded that, thanks to all those years, there was no hiding anything from him.

"Nothing." She sent him a faint smile. "Just a little homesick."

"A lot of memories in that old place," he consented with a thin smile of his own.

The place he'd claimed as his own when he moved to Knoxville. The place he'd taken her when she was a girl, where they'd sat on the floor alongside the shelves beneath the window, looking through his collection of paperbacks. The place where she'd come to him, seventeen and green and wanting him; where he'd pressed her down into the couch and showed her the meaning of pleasure. The place where he'd left her sobbing. The place he'd reclaimed for her, when they were man and wife. The place they'd brought their baby home to.

She felt the tears building at the backs of her eyes. "It's stupid, I know," she said in a small voice. "But it wasn't just an apartment…"

"No it wasn't." He'd grown serious. "I'm sad to leave it, too."

She reached for him…

And his phone rang, shattering the moment.

Mercy leaned over the side of the bed to dig it out of his jeans pocket. He held it up over his face, read the screen, frowned, and let it drop to the carpet.

More alert now, Ava propped up on an elbow. "Who was that?"

Mercy looked disgusted. "Colin."

"Colin…."

"O'Donnell."

It had been a year since their honeymoon in New Orleans, but the name O'Donnell hadn't faded from memory. She still saw Evangeline's tear-stained face in her nightmares, as the woman begged forgiveness for a betrayal Ava could never excuse.

She sat up, pushing her hair back. "Larry and Evie's son?" she asked, shocked.

Before he could answer, the phone started to ring again.

"Is that him?"

"Probably." Mercy shrugged, expression dismissive. "Whatever."

"Do…" Her mind was spinning. "Do you know what he wants?"

"I dunno. I didn't listen to all his messages."

"*All* of his messages?" She felt a swift, certain dread, and couldn't explain it. "Merc, how many times has he called you?"

"Like…" He squinted at the ceiling. "Ten, maybe? Something like that."

"Mercy!"

"What?" He shot her an annoyed frown.

"You…" She groped for the right words, wanting to insult him and shield him at the same time. All too well she remembered his mother, the notorious Miss Dee with her diseased paper-thin skin and her ugly laughter, mocking them. "Like father like son…" According to her, Remy Lécuyer – the original one – had fathered a child by his best friend's wife. Mercy had refused to entertain the notion that he had a half-brother – his father would never have done that. But a part of Ava feared the evil old hag had been right.

She took a breath and started over, calmer this time. "*Usually*, if someone calls you *ten times*, they have something to say to you."

He made a give-a-damn noise in the back of his throat. "I ain't seen the guy in twenty years. What's he want with me?"

Ava plucked at the decorative gold piping on the topsheet, struggling for delicacy. "Well, his dad did die…"

At the business end of Mercy's shotgun.

23

He stiffened all over, rigid with sudden, violent anger. "His dad died because he's was a fucking traitor bastard. And if anybody thinks I ought to apologize–"

Ava shook her head, hand upraised in a defenseless pose. "No, baby," she said quietly. "I don't think you ought to apologize."

Some of the energy bled out of him; he was too tired to be properly furious. But his gaze was wary. "No?"

She smiled softly. "No."

Because he was her darling monster, and she didn't care if he played by anyone else's rules. She'd married a professional torturer, and she had no illusions about that.

He settled further, letting his head rest back on the pillow. "I can't help Colin," he said, tone reflective. "I don't want to talk to him."

Ava slid down so she lay beside him. "Then you don't have to."

When the phone rang a third time, she ignored it, burrowing through the sheets so she could lay against his side. But inwardly, she worried. If the old ghosts of New Orleans were stirring, it was Mercy who stood to be hurt the most by them.

Holly couldn't sleep. She should have been able to: she was exhausted, and it was late, and dark, and the ceiling fan above them whirled lazily, the breeze cool across her skin. She lay on her side, one arm curled protectively around the slight roundness of her belly. Michael was behind her; he'd tucked her in close, so they fit like spoons, and his arm was heavy and lifeless across her waist, his breath even against the back of her head.

He wasn't asleep either, though. She could tell.

"Uncle Wynn was asking about names today," she said quietly, afraid to shatter the dark.

His hand shifted, settled over her belly, showing he knew what she was talking about. "I already told you I don't care," he said, not unkindly. "Pick out something you like."

Holly twitched a small smile. She knew he didn't care, because she knew that, for him, it was all about the baby, and the name was just a word he'd come to find meaningful, once there was a face to put to it.

She swallowed the nervous lump in her throat and said, "I thought, at first, maybe, about naming her after your mom. Mine too. Both of them. Camilla Lila."

"That's awful," Michael said, and she laughed.

"Yeah, kinda. But she could have a cute nickname. No one uses middle names unless they're scolding, anyway."

He was silent a moment behind her, then said, "Just name her after your mother if you want. *Camilla* never brought any luck to Mama."

She loved the way he said *Mama*, the rough deep edge to his voice; the wound was still raw, all these years later. And he was a secure enough man to remember her as Mama, and not "my mother."

Holly covered his hand with hers, fingers sliding into the grooves between his knuckles. "*Lila* isn't exactly a lucky charm, either."

Two dead mothers, killed at the hands of their husbands. What if their names proved curses, instead of legacies?

Michael's breath stirred her hair. "Give her her own name, then. Fresh start. No bad memories."

She nodded, and squeezed his hand.

That's what the baby would be – a fresh start. A perfect, unblemished life escaped out from under the pall of death that had brought her parents together. A chance for them to shift the cosmic balance, steal a little bit of grace from the tattered remnants of their own hearts.

Three
Louis Lécuyer's Nose

Remy was, according to the older, kid-experienced old ladies, a calm baby. He smiled a lot, and slept well. He ate like a champ. But when he cried, he could wake the dead. Why Ava had expected anything less from Mercy's offspring, she didn't know. Loud, boisterous men, she'd learned, sired children with healthy lungs who knew how to use them.

The baby monitor was sitting on the edge of the coffee table, but it wasn't necessary, because his sudden wail could be heard from all the way down the hall.

"I'll get him," Leah offered, surging to her feet. She was a little baby-crazy over him.

Sam sent her a wry grin from her spot on the floor. "Not sure you've got what he's after."

"I'll bring him back to his milk dispenser," Leah said with a laugh, blue-streaked ponytail swinging as she went around the corner.

Ava sat cross-legged on the living room rug as they all sorted through boxes. She shook her head at Leah's sprite-like effervescence. She was tee-minus-ten from a face-plant on the carpet and a nap; if not for the cheer and humor of the other girls, she wouldn't be able to keep her energy at an acceptable level.

To her left, Holly sorted the box full of Ava's desk contents, arranging tidy piles on the rug, each labeled with a Post-It note.

Sam was tackling kitchen boxes that had mistakenly been left in the living room and were too heavy to haul, emptying them and then toting the items to their proper place in the kitchen. As Leah returned with a squirming Remy in her arms, Sam sucked in a breath and reached deep into the bottom of her current box, drawing out a thick folder.

"This says 'Manuscripts.' " She smiled and showed Ava the front of the folder. "Are these all your old stories?"

"Ugh." Ava reached to accept the unhappy burden of her son with a fast smile for Leah. "Do you guys mind?" she asked, gesturing to the front of her flannel shirt.

"No," three voices said in chorus, and she discreetly thumbed open the buttons, adjusted her bra and fitted Remy to her breast. He latched on and it was, as always, a sudden shock to feel his determination.

Sam held the folder open in her lap, turning the pages with delicate care, long fingers barely touching the edges, sunlight burnishing her dark blonde hair to a rich gold. Fine, baby hairs floated away from the crown of her head, haloing her face. "God, you've written a ton," she said in an awed voice. "I feel supremely inadequate looking at this."

"It's all shit," Ava assured her. "Mostly me being emo during undergrad, all my broken heart rambling."

Sam glanced over with a knowing half-smile and snorted. "While you and Mercy were apart, I take it?"

She'd told Sam some of her romantic history. Organic girl talk, as they'd studied in the student center and slowly began to relax around one another; to find a true friendship that went beyond the classroom. Sam had gone to high school with Aidan – even if he'd been too up his own ass to notice the quiet girl with the glasses in the front row – and so Samantha Walton felt like a natural addition to Ava's small social circle.

Ava nodded, embarrassment warming her cheeks.

"Is it fiction?" Holly asked. She looked thoroughly interested.

"Yeah. Except, if anyone who knows me reads it, they'll realize what a whack-job I am."

Leah rolled her eyes. "Too late. We already know that."

"I'd love to read some of your writing," Holly said, and one glance at her earnest expression proved she meant it.

Ava frowned inwardly. "Well…"

Sam continued to flip through Ava's regrettable fictional choices. "This one's called '*Mon Amour.*' " She waggled her brows. "Is it steamy?"

"I know for a fact you don't like steamy fiction," Ava said, "and no. It's just sad and emo, like I said."

"Can I read it?" Sam asked with a hopeful smile, already in the process of unclasping the folder's rings so she could draw the pages out.

"You had two stories published in that magazine," Leah said. "And those were sad and emo, too."

Ava snorted. "Sure, what the hell. Have at 'em."

Sam clutched "*Mon Amour*" to her side and passed the folder to Holly. "Here, you pick something, Holly."

Bless Sam; she had been instantly sensitive to Holly's shyness and hesitancy, and had treated her with the utmost kindness, without coddling. Ava knew more than anything, Holly just wanted to be one of the girls, and not the one handled with kid gloves.

"There was one you told me about," Leah said, perching on the arm of the couch, thin legs swinging. She had on hot pink tube socks and white cotton cheerleading shorts. "The one about the ghost?" Her brows went up hopefully.

Ava sighed. "It's in there. 'Cadence.' "

Holly, a few pages in one hand, closed the folder and handed it up to Leah.

Remy had gone slack and sleepy in her arms, and when he released her nipple, she eased him up onto her shoulder, small pats on his back until he let out a soft burp.

"You want me to take him back?" Leah asked.

Ava was about to say no – she loved the warm baby-smell coming off the top of his head, the brush of the black downy hair on his scalp. But then the doorbell rang.

"Yeah, that'd be good." She handed Remy to Leah and got to her feet.

"Your boob's still hanging out," Leah said, helpfully.

"Thanks."

She did up the front of her shirt, pushed loose strands of hair back over her ears, and went to see who was at the door. Probably not the neighbors, she reflected, given the looks they'd been shooting her biker moving crew the day before. She hoped it wasn't them, anyway; she was in tattered old cutoffs, barefoot, the gator tattoo on her left foot dark and noticeable.

She looked through the window first, and saw a tall, tan, dark-headed man on her front porch. Very tall. Almost Mercy tall. The sleeves were cut out of his shirt, and she could see the ridges of veins beneath his golden skin. Long ropy forearms and heavy biceps. He had big hands, and he wore his jeans very tight, just loose enough at the bottoms to go over the tops of old Timberland work boots.

Her stomach lurched, like it was *her* belly full of milk and not Remy's. The first stirrings of dread raised the fine hairs on her arms, set her pulse to pounding in her ears. Whoever this man was, the way he carried himself was too familiar.

He turned and saw her through the window, waved, flashed her a smile. Tilted his head toward the door, asking her to open it.

That smile.

"Oh, God," she whispered.

Her hands were shaking as she turned the deadbolt and opened the door a fraction, wedging herself into the opening the same way she'd seen her mother do, a physical barrier. *This is my house, and I'm the*

28

queen, and you'll come in only if I want you to. She had to tip her head back to meet the man's gaze, something she was well-accustomed to.

Their faces weren't identical; there were subtle differences. This man's jaw was a little wider, his forehead broader, his brows more heavily slanted. His eyes were dark, but so were lots of people's. And though the hair was that same silken black, he wore it clipped short; much more respectable.

It was the nose that was irrefutable proof. Smiling dark eyes looked down the length of a narrow, autocratic nose. She recognized it from the faded photos. From the daily sight of the same noise on her beloved's face. There was a man standing on her doorstep with Louis Lécuyer's nose, and his name sure as hell wasn't Felix.

Mercy's half-brother.

Dee Lécuyer hadn't been lying. The bitch.

"Well hey there," he said, and the Cajun accent she knew so well came rolling off his tongue. Deep voice. Similar voice.

Ava broke out in a cold sweat all over.

He gave her a dazzling smile. It wasn't right – that was Mercy's smile. Where did he get off using it?

"I'm looking for somebody," he said, "and maybe you can help me, sweetheart." Boyish tilt to his head, twinkling eyes.

So this was what Mercy must look like to other women. She'd never been on the other side of this sort of thing; she'd been in love with Merc before she was old enough to know what flirting was.

She realized she still hadn't said anything, was standing with her mouth slack like an idiot, and gave herself a shake. When she spoke, she was surprised to hear the bite in her voice.

"You're looking for Mercy." When his brows went up, she said, "Er…Felix. Right?"

He gave her another grin. "Felix Lécuyer, that's the one. Does he live here?"

She narrowed her eyes. Him showing up at their door like this was unnerving; the alarms were pinging in the back of her mind. "How could you possibly know that? We just moved in yesterday."

"We…? Oh!" His eyes sprang wide and he coughed a short laugh. "Jesus Christ. *We?* You're her, then. You're his little girl." He folded his arms and leaned against the doorframe, close enough that she took a step back, and was forced to open the door wider. "Shit," he said, laughing again. "Mom said you were just a little jailbait thing, but I didn't think Felix would really go for that. Goes to show you never really know a guy, do you?"

Ava choked down her initial response and prayed for a dose of her mother's queenly grace. She shut her eyes a second – see Maggie, be Maggie – and then opened them again, lifting her chin at what she hoped was an imperious angle.

"I'm assuming you're Colin?"

Another blazing grin. "That's me, sweetheart."

"Alright, Colin." She pulled on her snappiest, coldest, most-educated voice. The I-watch-too-much-BBC voice. "Several things. For starters, age of consent in Tennessee is eighteen, so not jailbait."

His smile flared, and then began to dim as her list continued.

"Second, unless I'm mistaken, you haven't seen Felix in twenty years, so you know nothing about our relationship, or him either, for that matter. Third, I met gators down in your swamps with better manners than to show up unannounced and begin insulting their hostesses. And fourth, I have no idea how you got this address, so you've got some explaining to do."

His cheeks colored, faintly; his smile was quietly mocking, and genuinely amused at the same time. "You've got some claws on ya, huh?"

"Oh, you have no idea."

Growing serious, his smile still in place, but his eyes penetrating, he said, "I hear you saved Felix."

"I'll do it again if I have to." She wanted him to read the threat in her eyes, and thought that he did.

He held her gaze a moment, then glanced away, across the yard, toward the Jeep he'd left in the driveway. When he looked at her again, he'd composed himself, chastened and polite. "Can I come in?"

Ava heard Leah step up behind her. "Who is it? Are we gonna have to shoot him?"

"Maybe," Ava said, filled with warmth toward her friend. To Colin: "What do you want?"

"A word with Felix."

"He's at work. He won't be home 'til five-thirty."

Colin shrugged. "I can wait." When she frowned at him, he lifted both hands in a defenseless gesture. "You won't even know I'm here. I swear."

Still frowning, feeling like it was a terrible decision, she opened the door wide and stepped back, nearly colliding with Leah. "Leave your boots by the door, please."

He gave her another broad smile. "Yes, ma'am." And shucked his boots before stepping into the foyer.

This is a terrible idea, Ava berated herself.

As if he agreed, Remy let out another pealing scream.

Ava turned to take him from Leah, knowing he needed a diaper change, and caught Colin's wide-eyed interested look.

"Yours?" he asked, nodding to the baby.

"Mine and Mercy's."

Beside her, Leah was staring at Colin with horrified interest. "Oh my God. He looks–"

"Yeah," Ava said.

"Is he–"

"Yeah."

Holly and Sam were still on the floor when they walked into the living room, but not trying to be coy. They stared with open surprise and curiosity. As if scripted, both gasped at the sight of Colin.

So she wasn't imagining the resemblance, Ava thought. That was good.

She shifted Remy up onto her shoulder and raised her voice to be heard above his crying. "Colin, these are my friends: Leah, Holly, and Sam. Girls, this is Colin O'Donnell. Mercy's brother."

Colin looked much too at home on her sofa, sipping tea from one of her mismatched mugs, long legs stretched out in front of him. She'd put a kettle on – after Leah unearthed it from its box – in the hopes that something so domestic would drive Colin out to wait in his Jeep. Instead, he'd jovially accepted a cup and planted himself on the couch, asking each of them questions, keeping up light chitchat.

Holly was the last to leave, and she lingered at the front door, touching Ava lightly on the arm. "Should I stay?" she whispered. "I can."

Ava smiled. "No, I'll be fine. Mercy should be home any minute."

Eyes widening, Holly nodded. "Right. Be careful." She left in a hurry, and Ava didn't blame her. Judging by Mercy's clipped tone over the phone when she'd called to tell him Colin was here, it wasn't going to be a pretty reunion between the brothers.

Ava closed the door and returned to the living room, frowning at the sight of Colin's socked feet up on the coffee table. His gaze was fixed on Remy, who was staring back at the man from his swing, eyes never swerving as the motor rocked him forward and back.

"Serious little guy, isn't he?" Colin asked.

She snorted. "Maybe he's overcome by the family resemblance."

He glanced at her, a fast darting of eyes, a tightening of his expression; it furthered the likeness to Mercy. "About that…you keep saying 'brother.' Not sure I like that."

"Not sure you have a choice in it. Have you looked in a mirror lately?"

He grinned, but it didn't go to his eyes. "All the time, darlin', but I ain't laid eyes on Felix in a long time, so wouldn't do me much good there."

She leaned against the wall; she was exhausted from the move, and the day's sorting, and the last thing she wanted was the big blow-up about to happen.

"So you're in denial," she said. "That's original. Evie didn't tell you the truth?"

He stiffened, a subtle shift in energy toward something darker. Something Lécuyer. "You wanna say something about my mama?"

"No. I already said my piece to her face. Trust me – I don't want to think the worst of my father-in-law." Even if he was long dead. "But you look so much like my husband it's scary. The truth is, Colin, if your mother is insisting Larry O'Donnell was your biological father, she's lying to you."

He opened his mouth to say something –

And the growl of Mercy's Dyna echoed against the front of the house.

"Daddy's home," Ava said to Remy with false brightness. To Colin, she said, "I'd tread very carefully if I were you."

He scowled at her. "He's got some things to answer for."

"And you walked into something you can't hope to understand," she shot back. "Mercy isn't a goodtime Louisiana boy; he never was. You'd be smart to remember that."

The door off the mud room opened and Ava felt dread shoot through her. It made her lightheaded. She firmed up her shoulders, though, and called, "We're in here, baby." Then she listened to Mercy's slightly uneven footfalls as he walked through the kitchen, not bothering to take off his boots. When he appeared in the doorway, even she was a little taken aback.

Usually, when he was fresh from the garage, he had his cut pulled on over whatever ratty, stained t-shirt he'd worn to work that day. Dirty, windblown, dark from the sun, and smiling was how he greeted her every afternoon, stooping low to kiss her lips and the top of Remy's head.

Today, though –

32

He'd traded his undershirt for a black wifebeater that put his arms on impressive display. His cut shone softly with the glow of well-loved, carefully buffed leather, all his patches seeming more insistent than normal. *Knoxville, TN* over his breast pocket; *Tennessee* arcing beneath the lower pocket; the little embroidered knife patch with the bloodied tip, showing he'd shed blood for his club; *BH* for Baskerville Hall, to indicate that he'd fought with his London brothers; *HH* for hellhound, because he had earned special notoriety for violence and ruthlessness within the club; the fleur-de-lis, because he'd come from NOLA.

His black hair was pulled back in the front, and fell down past his shoulders, highlighting the lean angles of his face, the dark hollows around his eyes, the sharp blade of the Lécuyer nose. Glints of silver: wallet chain, the bracelet Ava had given him for his birthday, grommets on his black boots. He looked giant and terrifying, and Ava echoed Colin's deep breath with one of her own.

Mercy heard it and turned, face softening. "*Fillette*," he greeted, laying a hand on her waist, giving her a quick kiss.

Then he straightened, folded his arms, and squared off from Colin. "Enjoying yourself, sitting on my couch?"

Colin grinned, but there was a certain strain to the expression. "Good to see you too, Felix."

"How'd you get my address?"

Colin hadn't answered that question for her, but now, he shrugged and said, "I went by your old place. The agent was there showing the apartment, and she said I could find you here."

Ava wanted to choke on the slam of betrayal. Real estate agents weren't supposed to give out info like that. Mercy's eyes cut toward her at the small sound she made, then returned to Colin.

"You could've come by the clubhouse, if you wanted to see me. Should have. But you came here, when it was just my old lady at home." And by the dark quality of his voice, that wasn't tolerable.

Ava was realizing, as she tried wildly to interpret Colin's animosity, that Mercy wasn't uncomfortable with the notion that he'd killed Colin's father. Fake father. Whatever. A sentiment very much like hatred was lifting off him in invisible shimmers; Ava thought if she touched his skin, he'd burn her — that was how enraged he was. She'd anticipated awkwardness and a host of other emotions, but not this hatred.

It was frightening to behold.

Colin gestured casually to Ava. "She coulda left me standing on the welcome mat."

Trying to pin it on her, was he? She scowled. "I was raised to take in family, even if they don't deserve it."

"Family," he scoffed. To Mercy: "She keeps talking about us being brothers."

Mercy snorted. "All my brothers have a black dog patch on their backs."

Colin studied him a moment, smile frozen and insincere. "That's right. You moved away from the swamp and forgot all about the people you knew growing up, right? Nothin' but the brotherhood now. Fuck some old man who used to fish with you. Might as well put a shotgun in his belly."

Mercy took an aggressive step into the room. "Were you there?" His voice was deadly-calm. "Huh? Were you there the day that 'old man' brought a murderer to my door, so he could kill me and do...God knows what the fuck to my wife?"

Colin sat forward. "He wouldn't do that."

"Yeah? I used to think that, too."

Face flushing with anger, Colin's hands twitched on his knees, like he wanted to do something with them. He held his ground on the couch, though. "My father," he said slowly, "wouldn't hurt children." Insulting glance thrown Ava's way.

"Oh, damn," Ava said under her breath.

Mercy took another step toward the couch, spine bowing up, furious energy whipping through him, visibly tightening all the exposed muscles in his arms. He looked every inch the crossroads devil hound, come to collect a debt. "What in the hell," he said slowly, "is that supposed to mean?"

"I think you know."

"Merc," Ava said, and her voice brought him up short. She didn't misunderstand the way he leaned forward. If she didn't prevent it, he would drag Colin off the couch and inflict serious bodily harm to the man.

Colin, she saw by the sudden paleness of his face, didn't misunderstand either. He saw the aborted attack for what it was; his eyes cut to her and he saw her for what *she* was: the holder of the leash.

Ava took a deep, steadying breath. "Colin, I think you ought to go."

He scraped together a little indignation. "I need to–"

"Talk? Do it tomorrow. Go by Dartmoor on Mercy's lunch break. You guys can hash things out. But not here. Not now."

Mercy made a good show of collecting himself. He jerked a stiff nod toward the front door. "You heard the lady. You come find me tomorrow if you wanna talk." It wasn't a friendly invitation.

Colin got to his feet, face twisted with suppressed fury. "You killed my father," he said, coldly, quietly.

"Tomorrow," Mercy bit out.

Colin slammed the door in his wake, knocking askew the framed family photo Ava had hung in the foyer that morning.

Mercy walked to straighten it, tipping the frame to the side with one delicate finger. Then turned to face her. "So what's for dinner?"

"I didn't know you hated him," Ava said, as she carved the grocery store rotisserie chicken Sam had left for them in the fridge.

Mercy sighed elaborately. He sat at the table, divested of cut, holding Remy. It always melted her insides, the sight of those large, ruthless hands cradling the fragile little body with such reverence and care.

"I don't," he said, frowning to himself. "I mean, I didn't use to."

"It's been a year since Larry…" She didn't say it, arranging the meat on plates for them. "So Evie must have finally told him what happened."

"Or he's just now getting around to caring about it," Mercy said with a snort. "You gotta understand something about Colin – he's a total fucking waste of space."

Ava bit back a grin. "Do tell."

Warmed to his topic, Mercy pulled on his storyteller voice with obvious relish. "Colin's a little bit younger than me, but we were close enough that Daddy and Larry pushed us into being friends when we were kids. Colin went to school – real school – and I didn't, so" – he shrugged – "Daddy and Gram thought I needed a friend."

Much the same way her own parents had worried about her lack of a social life growing up. Thank God for Leah.

"But Colin was a little shit. He was bigger than all his friends, and he pushed them around; they were all scared of him, and they did what he wanted and pretended it was fun. Taunting homeless people; shoplifting; throwing rocks at cars that went past. Nothing too evil, I don't guess, but just…shitty. I saw him cut a girl's ponytail clean off once."

35

"He was a bully," Ava said, disturbed by the notion that someone who looked so much like her husband could be so different.

Mercy nodded. "And when he got older, he was aimless. Never holds down a job for more than a few weeks; gets fired from most. He sneaks out of women's windows in the middle of the night and never calls them. His folks have needed a new roof on their house for years, and he never offers to give them a dime. Not that he's got one to his name." He pulled a disgusted face. "He's just a dickhead loser."

"That was sort of the impression I got," she said. They would make sandwiches, she decided, since she couldn't locate half her pots. She pulled out bread, lettuce and mustard from the fridge. "But I didn't expect you to be so upset that he was here."

He was staring at Remy's face. The baby was giving him an owlish look from the crook of his father's arm. "I didn't expect it either," he admitted. "I just was."

He seemed to shake himself and glanced at her as she assembled their sandwiches. "What about you, though. Seemed like you were awful pissed at him."

She lowered her face over the plates, not wanting him to see her eyes. "I was. I am."

He cleared his throat in an invitation for her to explain.

Carefully, she said, "I thought him showing up unannounced like that might bother you. And I didn't want that."

"I thought you just said you didn't expect it to upset me."

"Upset you *that much*."

When she glanced up, he was starting at her, brows drawn together, and she sighed. "I know you don't want to think the worst of your father."

"I don't."

"Even if your half-brother is living proof that he–"

"That asshole isn't my half-anything," he said with finality. "Daddy would never have done that."

Ava started to argue, and changed her mind. Let Colin be the bad guy here, she decided. "You're right," she said, lifting their plates. "Let's eat."

Four
Sins of the Father

The ropes again. Biting into her wrists, pulling her arms at unnatural angles. The bed again. The sheets damp from sweat, clinging to her skin. The room again. Her father again. His hands again, sliding up the bare smooth length of her thigh.

And then, as shocking as a bucket of cold water dumped across her exposed body, her own face, hovering above her, alongside her father's. She saw herself, naked and scarred, the old rope burns at her wrists inflamed and red.

"Don't fight." She heard her own voice, saw her own lips move. "It's over faster if you don't fight."

And then she realized what was happening. She wasn't in her own body, but in that of her daughter. She glanced through her child's eyes, up at herself, a compliant bystander as Abraham Jessup reached her hip and smoothed his rough hand across her belly.

"No!" she screamed, lurching against her bonds. The ropes didn't hold, and her arms shot forward. She surged up off the bed, reached with curled fingers for Abraham's face, sharp-tipped claws going for his eyes.

"Jesus Christ!" It wasn't her father's voice, cursing in the dark. And they weren't his hands, she realized, as they curled around her wrists and held her back.

Her eyes opened.

For real this time.

"Hol. Holly! Wake up!"

She was not in the old farmhouse, in that awful bed where her mother had died; where her father, uncle, and cousin-husband had violated her body, heart, and soul.

She was in her new home: the Craftsman in Knoxville, with the brick and concrete porch and the shag carpet. The place she lived with Michael. Her husband, who knelt on the bed in front of her, holding her arms, holding her at bay when she would have gouged his face with her nails.

It was only a dream. A nightmare. Sparked by the feel of Michael's hand on her skin.

"Wha...what..." She panted. Tears filled her eyes, distorting the shadowed bedroom and Michael's silhouette in front of her. She knew it was him now – his smell, the sound of his voice, the energy

37

pulsing off of him. But the nightmare still had tendrils wrapped round her.

She sucked in a deep breath and started again. "Oh, God. What time is it? What…"

"It's eleven," he said. "I just got home."

Home from the club run he, Ghost, and Walsh had headed off for that morning. Something so wrapped up in Lean Dogs' secrecy that he could only tell her he'd be back later, and not to wait up for him. She'd waited for a while; she hated going to bed alone. But finally, the exhaustion of pregnancy had drawn her to bed, and she'd succumbed to some of the worst nightmares she'd had since meeting Michael.

"Oh," she said stupidly, and all the energy drained out of her in a great rush, leaving her dizzy and weak. "Right." She started to shake.

"Jesus," Michael repeated, a whisper this time. He was nothing but a shadow in the dark of their bedroom, but when he bundled her into his chest, she could smell the soap on him, feel the warmth of his bare skin. She hadn't heard him come in or shower, but was grateful for the feeling of him naked against her now, in the wake of terror.

He didn't ask her what she'd dreamed of; he knew. He smoothed her hair back, let his fingers work gently through its tangles as his arms supported her.

It felt like a long time before her shaking subsided and she was able to draw in a deep breath. The thing she hadn't been foolish enough to say in the daylight came falling off her tongue now. "I'm not ever going to be normal."

He snorted, breath rustling through her hair. "Who the hell's normal?"

"Lots of people," she said against his chest. "You ought to be normal if you're going to be someone's mother."

"Fuck, Hol…" He eased her back, hands on her arms, far enough so she could see the faint glimmer of his eyes through the dark. She thought she could make out the grim set of his mouth. "Alright, look. Your friend Ava – is she normal?"

"Well…"

"Or is she the weird kid who's been obsessed with Mercy her whole life?"

"That's not fair."

He made a disagreeing sound.

"It's not," she insisted. "Ava has a mom – she has a whole family. She's been to school. She has things together–"

"Which is why she ran off to the swamp with Mercy last year, right? Because all her shit's together?" he asked, dryly. "Sweetheart, you don't know how normal or abnormal anyone is. That's not something people go around telling the world about."

He gave her a little shake. "We've talked about this before. You never did anything awful; you survived awful. How's a kid get a better mother than that?"

"But what if…what if I'm not strong enough to protect her?"

Michael took a deep breath. "From what?"

"Everything."

He had no answer for that. They sat facing one another, quiet in the dark, his hands warm on her arms.

"Sorry," Maggie said when Holly jumped, and Holly shook her head, berating herself mentally for startling so easy.

"No, I wasn't – it's fine," she assured with a forced smile, glancing up at the MC first lady standing in front of her desk. "Can I help you with anything?"

Maggie set the cardboard box she held on the front of the desk and propped her hands on her hips, head tilting as she gave Holly a nerve-wracking once-over. She, as always, made a plain white tank top and holey jeans look chic; might have had something to do with the high-heeled sandals and the rattling bangle bracelets, but mostly was because of the aura of authority that seemed to radiate around her shining blonde head.

"You look tired," she said, and it was neither an insult, nor a show of concern.

Holly tried another stiff smile. "A little. Guess it's a side effect of–" She gestured to her stomach.

Maggie nodded and picked up the box again, stepping around the desk, going to the file cabinets at Holly's back. "Yeah," Maggie agreed. "Growing a human being is exhausting."

Sound of cabinets pulling open with metallic clicks and whooshes.

"You feeling alright otherwise?" Maggie asked, tone casual.

Holly still felt shaky with the chief old lady. She was observant enough to know that Maggie was only truly casual with her blood relations, but not in-the-know enough to figure out the woman's true feelings toward her.

"The morning sickness is gone, thankfully," Holly said, pivoting her spinning chair around. She didn't like to have her back to people, for the most part. "I don't have a great appetite, but at least I stopped throwing up."

Maggie nodded to herself, slotting file folders from the box into the drawers she'd opened. "Always a good stage. You know, Nell said she wasn't ever sick, not during one of her three pregnancies. The bitch," she said with a quick, playful smile sent Holly's way. "Some girls have all the luck."

"Hmm." Holly moved her hand absently to rest against her stomach.

"You picked out a name yet?"

Why was that the thing everyone wanted to know?

"No."

"You've still got plenty of time." It was said in a comforting way. "I took forever to come up with 'Ava.' And then I almost didn't use it, because that meant two Teague kids with A names. But..." She shrugged and pushed the drawers back in. "That was just her name, you know? I couldn't imagine anything else."

Holly nodded. She was hoping that would happen. That suddenly a name would bloom to life inside her mind, and the baby would become that much more real to her, not just a little girl, but a girl she'd named.

Maggie lifted the box up over her head, stretching upward to slide it onto the top of the cabinet. "These are old receipts that wound up in the wrong office," she explained. "I don't have time to file them all now, but..."

Holly wasn't paying attention. Maggie's shirt had ridden up and revealed a tattoo just on the inside of one hip. Its black ink slightly faded from time, a realistic paw print marked her skin, as large as the print of a big dog, complete with little triangles of claws on the ends of the toe pads. Beneath it, in flowing script, *Ghost*.

As quick as the tattoo had appeared, it was covered, Maggie tugging the hem of her shirt down as she lowered her arms.

Holly felt a sting of guilt as she looked up and met the woman's gaze.

But Maggie didn't seem offended. "All the old ladies have one," she said, then frowned. "Though I guess Ava doesn't, since she got pregnant so fast. Guess you don't either, for that matter."

Holly's stomach knotted. "Am I supposed to have one? Is it important?"

Maggie shrugged. "It's just the way things have always been done. Michael hasn't said anything about it to you?"

"No." Doubt prickled up the back of her neck. "Should I bring it up?"

Maggie's gaze was measuring, even if her words were kind. "You can. I mean, you can't get a tat while you're pregnant – it's not recommended, anyway. But you can ask if he wants you to have one later. After."

"He…he must want that. Since I'm his old lady. And that's what old ladies do…"

Maggie shrugged again as she headed for the day. "All you can do is ask."

When she was gone, Holly turned slowly back to the desk, her stomach feeling empty above the solid weight of the growing baby. Michael wasn't one for doing things strictly the MC way. At least, he hadn't been before she'd come into his life. Taking her on as his old lady had him searching out his brothers for a newborn, awkward comradery. For her sake, he was making an effort to be something besides a knife within the club. For her, he was working on his caveman social skills.

But he'd never mentioned the tattoo.

Maybe he had no interest in inking his name into the hip of a woman who bolted out of bed and tried to claw his eyes out in the middle of the night.

"The paw print?" Ava asked with a small frown as she lifted plates up into the proper cabinet, adding them to the stack already there.

Holly stood at the counter opposite her, slotting silverware into a rack in a drawer. They were getting the kitchen all set up and ready for use while Remy took his afternoon nap.

Maggie had suggested she close up the office early, re-routing any truck rental calls to the main office. "Go home and get some rest," she'd said. Holly hadn't argued, but she hadn't gone home, instead heading for the Lécuyers' new house, thinking Ava might like more help. She'd been ushered in with a welcome smile.

Ava took the next plate from the box and stared at it in contemplation, tilting it so the sunlight skimmed down its shiny yellow surface. "Mercy and I've never talked about it." It sounded like an admission. "We just…" She glanced up at Holly, still frowning. "We both have our gators." Holly had noticed the new tat on Mercy's neck. "And we…I guess we weren't thinking too much about tradition. Or the club." Her frown became a rueful half-smile. "We were all about our own thing."

And their thing was beautiful, from all outward appearances.

41

Holly nodded. But there was still a knot in her gut. "Do you think I ought to ask Michael–"

"No," Ava said quickly. She seemed to shake out of her trance and put the plate away, reached for the next one. "Not that I'm trying to tell you what to do," she amended with a fast glance as she worked. "I don't know Michael as well as you do, I know that. But if things are going well, then why mess it up because of something like a tattoo?"

"Well," Holly countered, "if things really are as good as I think they are, could a tattoo actually make a mess?"

"Good point," Ava said.

Holly wanted to twist her hands together, and reached for a bundle of forks instead, arranging them in their slot. "The thing is, though, I don't know if things are good."

Ava paused, facing her fully, eyes bright with sympathy. "You guys are having trouble?"

"No – no, not trouble. It's only…" She didn't think she could bring herself to confide any of her history to Ava. She heaved a deep sigh. "I haven't ever…I don't know if…Michael's the only relationship I've ever had," she finished in a rush. "I don't know what normal looks like or feels like. I had a really bad nightmare last night, and I freaked out, and I thought he was someone else, and I sort of attacked him–" She had to suck in a desperate breath. Sweat was forming on top of her skin, under her clothes, nervous perspiration. "He was really quiet this morning, and I don't know if he's…what if he starts to rethink marrying me?"

"Holly," Ava scolded softly. "He's not going to do that."

"Everything happened fast with us. I never expected him to marry me. Or to be okay with the baby." She clamped her lips shut before her voice started to shake.

Ava's expression was half-sad, half-thoughtful. "Michael isn't exactly normal, in my book. I don't think you need to worry about him. This nightmare. He knows what it was about?"

Holly nodded.

"That's all you can do, then, is talk to him. Trust him." She gave her an earnest look. "He's not the kind of guy who'd marry for the hell of it. He loves you. You know he does."

Holly nodded.

They worked in silence a few moments, Holly wishing she could make sense of the tangled worries lodged in her throat, hating that she'd admitted her doubts to her friend. That's what friends were for, sure, but Holly didn't want to have said doubts in the first place.

After a while, Ava said, "You know, you guys didn't really get a chance to bask in being together." When Holly glanced up, she said, "You were recovering when you got married, and then you found out you were pregnant. It did happen fast. Doesn't mean it wasn't good – just fast. Maybe you two need to spend a little more time together."

"Like a vacation?" She didn't know if either of them could get time off from work.

Ava grinned. "Like, stay in bed for days and do nothing but talk and have sex."

Holly felt her cheeks warm. "Oh."

Ava's grin widened. "Never underestimate the power of working things out in the bedroom."

By the time Michael got home from work that evening, a plan was starting to form in her head. It scared her a little, and left her breathless, too.

It was hot, so she made them chicken with cold pasta salad for dinner. She was slicing up iceberg lettuce for a true salad when she heard the garage door go up and then down, and Michael's booted footsteps came up the basement stairs. He was a lithe, graceful man; it was more the steps creaking under his weight than his feet making much noise. Still, it was enough for her to know it was him, and to be prepared for the basement door to open and close, emitting him into the room.

He put his back to her first, toeing off his boots and setting them in the rack by the door. Holly took the chance to look him over from behind, the strong, tapered lines of his back, the fit of his jeans, the lengths of his legs.

He was beautiful, and the sight of him in his dirty garage shirt added to the breathlessness of her plan.

"Hi," she called, hoping her voice sounded normal, casual.

"Hey." His expression was careful as he turned and walked toward her. He went to the fridge first, grabbed a beer for himself and twisted off the top. When he walked over to kiss her, it was a peck, and not the deep, tongue-laden greeting it normally was.

"Good day?" she asked.

"Yeah. You?"

"Mmhm."

He lingered beside her a moment, like he wanted to say something else, but awkwardness got the best of him and he headed into the living room.

Holly wanted to be crushed by this roadblock thrown up between them. But instead, she sliced through the lettuce with sure strokes of the knife, planning tomorrow night. It had to be then. She couldn't let things linger like this any longer than necessary.

Five
No Brother of Mine

Michael felt like an ass. Was that the right noun? Ass? He wasn't sure. All he knew was that he was about to do something he hadn't ever thought he'd do, and he wasn't too keen on it.

As he approached the open bay doors of the bike shop, it looked like he hadn't picked the best day for this errand.

"Motherfucking, cocksucking piece of shit…" There was a loud clang of a wrench falling onto the concrete and Mercy straightened up from the other side of the BMW bike he'd been kneeling in front of. Normally, it was his jovial side that came out to play in the garage, and not the dark Mr. Hyde part he kept under better wraps. But today, his face was all harsh angles, which made him look both thinner overall, and more threatening.

"Aidan," he called. "If you're gonna make me work on all this foreign shit, then you gotta leave me my good wrenches."

Aidan shouted something in response from across the garage that Michael couldn't make out.

"Damn punk-ass," Mercy grumbled under his breath. "Think you're the boss or some shit."

His head jerked, as if he'd suddenly heard or taken note of Michael's approach. His gaze lifted and it wasn't friendly. He took a deep breath, though, nostrils flaring, and he composed his voice into something polite. "You wanna swap places for the day? I'd kill to get away from this." He gestured to the bike.

Michael snorted. "I think Hol'd have a coronary when you walked in for dinner."

A slow smile eased the tightness in Mercy's features. "Wait. Was that…did you just crack a joke? Is that what I'm hearing?"

Michael dropped his head and stepped into the shade of the bay, grateful to find it a good ten degrees cooler out of the direct sunlight. The toes of his boots, he saw at this angle, were spattered with drying, gummy motor oil. Hmm…he'd have to buff that off or risk relegating this pair to yard work only.

Mercy was not one for making strained conversations more so – his social graces, in light of what he did for the club, were mind-boggling. "So what brings you all the way down to this end?" he asked as he resumed his crouch in front of the bike. Michael didn't miss the small grunt of discomfort that meant his bad knee was bothering him.

"I…" Michael cleared his throat. He hated this. But he could picture Holly's wild, moonlit eyes from two nights ago; he could feel the fragile wall of tension between them last night, the invisible barrier that had kept him on his side of the bed. He didn't like sleeping with any sort of distance, not now that he'd grown used to wrapping himself around his old lady. He hadn't had many nightmares since she'd come into his life.

Obviously, she couldn't say the same thing.

With a resolute sigh, he lifted his head, resting his hip against a tool chest. "I wanted to…get your opinion on something."

Mercy nodded as he worked, his large hands deft on the guts of the machine he studied. "If it's that Pontiac I saw get towed in this morning, my opinion is that it's a lost cause."

"No." Shit, why was this so difficult? "A personal opinion, I mean."

"About?"

"I'm thinking about getting an alarm system installed."

There. Now was that so hard?

Mercy glanced up at him from beneath raised brows. "An alarm system."

Michael folded his arms. "Yeah. One of the good ones. Name brand and shit."

Mercy watched him. "You have to be careful with that. Don't want the cops showing up the next time you lock yourself outta the house and find you dripping ill-gotten guns."

Michael nodded. It was a risk most of the brothers didn't take. When you wired your house up and invited a third party to monitor it and contact the police, you were inviting Big Brother into your home. Giving the cops an excuse to bust the lock, come right in, and start rifling through your shit in the name of searching for a burglar. It wasn't anything civilians ever had to worry about. But a one-percenter? That was a cause for concern.

"I thought," he said, wanting to fidget and holding still, "it might make Hol feel safer. She'd know no one but me coulda got in past it."

Mercy blinked and his expression became curious in a careful sort of way. "Who'd be going in there but you anyway?"

He flicked a glance across the garage, ensuring that Aidan and his prospect were all the way on the other side, locked in conversation about the Harley they worked on. He hadn't planned on telling Mercy any of the details – and he would never betray Holly's trust by talking about the dark, secret ones – but suddenly, he could sense a forthcoming relief in entrusting another man with his worry.

Is this what friendship felt like? Is that what was happening here with this goofus Cajun he hadn't ever expected to like?

"She's having nightmares," he said quietly. "And the other night, I spooked her." Understatement of the year. "I just…don't want her to worry so much."

Mercy didn't wave off the concern like one of his other brothers might have. Like, say, Ghost or Aidan would. Instead he nodded, and said, "Yeah." He made a thoughtful face. "She knows her way around a gun, right?"

"Of course."

Another nod. "That's all that makes me willing to leave Ava home by herself. Good locks on the doors? You could nail the windows shut."

Michael snorted. "She likes the fresh air."

"Yeah, well…sacrifices and all that."

But Michael could envision the shuttered woe in her pixie face as she stood back and watched him drive nails through the window sashes.

"Can I say something?" Mercy said. "And I swear I don't mean to be prying into your business. Just an observation."

Michael frowned, but nodded.

"Holly – if I'm right in assuming what I assume – has some deep shit to move past." His look was almost apologetic. "I think a lot of the time, you can't get past deep shit."

"Yeah. That's what I'm afraid of."

Mercy shrugged, and there was something polite about the way he refocused on the bike. "If it'll make her feel better, then get the alarm. You gotta take care of your girl first. Without her, there's nothing much worth caring about."

Exactly Michael's sentiment. "Thank you," he said, and meant it.

Colin hadn't showed up yet, and that was a good thing, but dread had Mercy's nerves stretched tight as fresh guitar strings. Michael's alarm system problems were a welcome distraction, so he asked the guy if he wanted to stick around a minute, render an opinion on this dumbass Beamer bike he was working on.

"Nothing's easy to get to," Mercy complained as they both crouched in front of the engine. "They never are, but this som'bitch is brand new, and it's even more fucked up."

Michael traced one of the gleaming coils with a finger, frowning. "I never understand why anyone would shell out this kinda money for something like this."

A sentiment with which Mercy wholeheartedly agreed. They weren't patched into an outlaw MC because they appreciated fine German engineering. "Rich dicks think they're cool."

Michael made a sound in the back of his throat to show what he thought of that.

Across the garage, there was a clatter as something was dropped.

Aidan and Carter said, "Jeeeeeesus," at the same time.

And Mercy knew the dreaded moment had come. Colin was here.

He stood, and saw the bastard standing just outside the garage, in the full sunlight. Aidan and Carter stared at him. Carter was actually pointing.

Aidan said, "Dude, are you…nah, can't be. Are you…?"

"He's looking for me," Mercy said, and the doofuses swiveled around, looking between the two of them.

"I think he *is* you," Aidan said. He grinned. "But I'm guessing you're the evil twin, bro."

"Stuff it." He turned and handed his favorite wrench to Michael, catching the guy's quietly startled expression. "Long story," he muttered, and then headed out to meet Colin before he could start charming the impressionable children.

"What do you want?"

All the fake cheer he'd put on display for Ava the other night was gone, replaced with a simmering anger that gave Mercy the eerie impression he was looking in a sideshow mirror. "Like I said before, I need to talk to you."

Mercy sighed. "Not here."

"You done yet?"

In answer, Mercy unwrapped the cling film off the second leftover chicken sandwich Ava had brown-bagged him for lunch and took a huge bite of it. He was enjoying setting the guy on edge. They'd walked over to the clubhouse, far enough from the bike shop that, should things devolve to punch-throwing, they wouldn't be doing it in front of paying customers. Mercy, in what he thought of as an inspired choice, had gone in, snagged his lunch, and was devouring it down to the last Dorito crumb, making Colin wait. He'd never done that when they were kids; it felt damn good.

To be a guy the ladies had always swooned over, Colin's sneer made him look truly ugly. "Did wifey make you lunch?"

"Yep."

"Did she write you a love note on your napkin?"

It said *Love you bunches, Monster*, with three little hearts doodled off to the side. He'd crumpled it in his palm first thing when he'd opened the bag and stuffed it in his cut pocket when Colin wasn't looking. "Nope," he said, cramming the last square of bread in his mouth. "What's the matter?" he asked when he'd swallowed. "Wish she'd written one for you? All nostalgic for the good ol' days when your mama wiped your ass for you?"

Colin ignored the jab and said, "Nah, man, you were the one always starvin' for a mama."

Okay. Lunch was over.

Mercy shoved his bag and half-drunk soda off to the side of the picnic table where they sat, giving Colin a level look. "Say what you gotta say to me, and then fuck off. I don't have time for your bullshit."

Colin shrugged, and in a deceptively calm voice said, "A'ight. You wanna tell me why you put a round of buckshot through my old man?"

"Because he was a betraying son of a bitch. Next question."

Colin wasn't as cool as he wanted to be. The affectation dropped off his face, leaving his eyes flashing and his features clenched tight. Mercy didn't want to see the resemblance to his reflection in the guy…really, he didn't.

"They were taking care of you!" He jabbed a long forefinger across the table in Mercy's direction. "They brought you food—"

"And they brought the men chasing us straight to our doorstep. They gave some hired PI our coordinates out there at Saints Hollow – they might as well have led him to us."

"Mom—"

"Evangeline's a liar and a bitch." *And maybe an adulteress too*, he added silently. "You think she gave you the real story?"

"I'm supposed to trust a goddamn biker instead?" There was a vein pounding in his temple, just beside the end of his eyebrow. It reminded Mercy, alarmingly, of his father Remy, the quiet wrath that had overtaken the big man's body on such rare occasion.

Mercy took a deep, steadying breath and let it out through his nostrils. Another. He forced his hands flat on the table. "Whether or not we hate each other, you know I always loved your folks. You *know* I did. When Dad and Gram–" He broke off, the words still jagged and painful in his throat, even after all this time. It wasn't the same, he wanted to tell Colin, because the guy had never loved his parents the way Mercy had loved his father and grandmother. The losses weren't on the same plane of grief. There was no comparison.

But instead, he said, "Larry and Evie were there for me, and whenever I needed them after that. I loved them," he repeated. "But" – tilt of his head, meaningful widening of his eyes – "there's love, and then there's *love*, and no one in the world is ever going to hurt my *fillette*. No way, no how. I would kill any man, woman, or God help me, child, that I had to, so I could keep her safe. All bets are off when it comes to Ava. I'd shoot the Virgin Mary in the face if I had to. Do you get that?"

Colin leaned back, hands braced on the edge of the table, nostrils flared as if he smelled something foul. "You're that pussy-whipped?"

Mercy felt a wide, humorless spread across his face. "She's my conscience. My soul. The only part of me that hasn't gone all the way dark. No one fucks with her and gets out alive."

It was silent a long, strained beat. A complicated sequence of emotions shifted across Colin's face. In a low voice, he said, "Dad wouldn't have hurt your little girl."

"The men he told about us would have, in a heartbeat."

Small frown. Then a larger one, growing in its conviction. "You killed my father."

"I had to."

Colin glanced away, muscle in his jaw twitching.

"So what are we doing here?" Mercy asked him. "Where is this going?"

"Honestly? I don't know. I expected you to deny it."

"Not big on lying."

Colin glanced over again, eyes hard, expression cold. "I ought to make you pay for it, Felix."

Mercy dipped his head. "You're welcome to try."

"It's not like I was showing it to her on purpose," Maggie said, digging through her takeout salad with the end of her fork, spearing a hunk of grilled chicken. "She just happened to see it. I wasn't trying to give her tattoo envy." The look she flashed up to Ava suggested she didn't appreciate having her motives questioned. And it reminded Ava that, ordinarily, she wasn't the one doing any questioning.

Ava swallowed down a moment's daughterly hesitation and adjusted Remy in her arms. "I know." The baby fussed and she lifted him higher. "But I think—" She didn't want to say this.

Maggie's brows lifted. *Go on.*

"I think you don't like Holly very much. And I don't really know why." And also, because there'd been a time in her life when her mother's opinion of someone was all she would have needed to make a judgment, but she'd found herself enjoying her small knot of friends. She liked softening the club in their eyes – knew that, when Leah and Sam and Holly were out in the world, they were thinking better things of the Lean Dogs.

Maggie sat back in her chair, salad abandoned. "I don't have a problem with Holly."

Ava gave her a *really?* look.

"I don't. I don't know her well enough to dislike her." Fractional narrowing of her eyes. "Just like I don't know her well enough to trust her blindly."

Ava blinked. "I don't trust anyone blindly. And whatever happened to Holly in her past life, she deserves a little kindness now, I think."

"Probably so."

"But you're testing her," Ava said, grimly.

Maggie tipped her head to the side. "This isn't a rainbows and puppy dogs life we lead, baby, and you know it. The problem is, let's say the cops come to ask questions, or that FBI jackass shows back up – and believe me, he's going to show back up. We have no idea how Holly would handle herself. She loves Michael; I don't doubt that for a second. But will she protect the club if she has to? Will she honor the brotherhood…and the sisterhood?"

Ava wanted to say "yes," but she couldn't, and Maggie knew that, her face softening.

"You can't drown a stranger in love and hope they take your side when the shit hits the fan, Ava. I've been around too long to think the best of people. The truth is: Until we know how much we can trust Holly, we can't peel back the curtain too far."

This conversation had taken a turn toward the unpleasant. Maggie wasn't wrong – but Ava didn't have to like the seeds of doubt being sown in her mind.

"Right." She pushed to her feet and bent to strap Remy into his carrier. "Well, I'd better get back to my closet organizer nightmare."

51

"Come on, I didn't offend you that much, did I?" Maggie protested.

A little bit. "No," she said with a quick smile as the buckles clicked into place, Remy snug within them. "I've still got a ton to do at the house."

"Ava."

"I'm not offended." She lifted the carrier. "I'll call you later on, okay?"

Maggie's lips pursed, as if she wanted to say more. But she nodded. And then she remembered something, sitting forward. "Oh, I forgot to mention. Your dad wants to have lunch with you one day."

Ava froze halfway to the door. "He *what?*"

Maggie nodded. "Yeah. He asked me to ask you – he wants just the two of you to go into town and have a real, sit-down, restaurant lunch together." She waved. "Which means Stella's, I'm sure. Or IHOP, something like that. You would have to take Remy, of course." Because of the breastfeeding. "But he's mentioned it to me more than once. It's pretty important to him."

"I…" Questions crowded her mind. There was a tight ball of dread gaining weight in her stomach. Ghost didn't ever just want to shoot the breeze with her. They didn't spend casual time together. If he was wanting to have lunch, there must be something catastrophic at play.

She dampened her lips. "Why didn't he ask me himself?"

"You know how he is. Mr. Awkward when it comes to the two of you." Maggie shoved her half-eaten salad to the side and her hands poised over the computer keyboard, ready to return to work. "But find an afternoon for it. Your daddy doesn't ask for this sort of thing often."

"Yeah, no kidding."

Feeling a little numb with surprise, Ava walked out into the sunshine-filled parking lot, immediately blanketed by the humid, summertime riverfront air that clogged the Dartmoor property from one end to the other. She shifted Remy's carrier to her left hand, slid her sunglasses into place with the right –

And caught sight of an unmistakable figure sitting at a picnic table in front of the clubhouse. Across from him was his equally unmistakable half-brother, and her numbness morphed into a kind of low-buzzing alarm. She didn't want to intrude on anything Mercy wanted to keep to himself, but she likewise didn't want to see the prospects out here power-washing blood off the concrete later. She would just check in, she decided.

Colin had his back to her, and as she approached, the tension across his shoulders, the way the tightening of his muscles created a particular scheme of shadows in the folds of his shirt, was so familiar. She got a look at Mercy's face – tight jaw, eyes squinted against the sun, brows throwing angular lines up on his forehead – and imagined that's what Colin's must look like now. The shoulders were the same, why not the faces too?

Mercy noticed her, and his face relaxed instantly as his eyes skipped over her. She saw his throat ripple as he swallowed. Nerves? Was he nervous about her approaching Colin? Yes, she decided, he was. He thought the other man was dangerous, and maybe she should have thought so too.

"Hi, baby," he greeted. "You visiting with Mags?"

Colin twisted around sharply, like he hadn't heard her coming and was startled to see her behind him.

"I was," she said. "Thought I'd come say hi before I headed home."

And then none of the three of them said anything else. There was never any awkwardness between the two of them in front of the rest of the Dogs. But that counted as family, and Colin – while blood family – was nothing of the sort when it came to love and loyalty.

The silence was thicker than the humidity.

Ava cleared her throat and it sounded like a gunshot. "Hello, Colin. How are you today?"

He gave her a sideways smile. "I'm just fine, darlin'. How 'bout you?"

"Good." She looked to Mercy. "Do you need anything before I go?" The silent question was: *You're not going to cause a scene, are you?*

"Nah, I'm good." He smiled the answer: *No guarantees, sweetheart.*

She tried to hide her frown. "Okay."

"Come here and gimme a kiss."

She did, setting Remy's carrier on the table and bracing a hand on Mercy's shoulder as she leaned down and pressed her lips to his. It didn't matter if she was above him; it always felt like he was the one kissing her, and she was the one receiving the tender attention instead of giving it.

When she pulled back, Mercy squeezed one of Remy's tiny socked feet, his face transformed a moment, all traces of stress leaving him. "Big Man," he greeted the baby, with a quiet smile.

Then his eyes went back to Colin, hardening, and Ava knew it was time to leave. Mercy didn't want her around the guy, and though

Colin had no power to hurt *her* emotionally, she wouldn't stress her husband further with her presence. Of all the things that gave the man nightmares, threats to her were the worst.

If she wanted to give Colin a piece of her mind, she'd have to do it by herself.

Six
These Ropes

"Hol?" Michael called as he stepped through the basement door into a cold kitchen. It was a shock: no happy sound of sizzling meat, no smell of onions and garlic, no chatter of the radio on the counter, no quietly humming wife reading the latest *Southern Living* as she waited for the oven to preheat.

Fear streaked through him. "Hol?" He shoved the door shut behind him and strode through the kitchen, not bothering to take off his dirty garage boots. "Holly?"

The living room, foyer, and never-used dining room were military tidy, wood surfaces gleaming with fresh polish, but still there was no sign of her.

His gut clenched tight, nausea ripping at the base of his throat as his heart turned into a kettle drum in his chest. What if something had...? What if someone...? What if she...? All the doors were locked, but stranger things had happened. Violent things had happened. And Holly here all alone, and terrified, and needing him. Oh God, if –

"Holly!" he shouted as he started down the hallway, almost jogging.

"I'm in here," her voice floated out of the master bedroom door, and he had to pause a moment, throwing out a hand to brace against the wall, sucking in a deep, painful breath.

"Jesus," he muttered. He'd been on the verge of cardiac arrest.

"Everything alright?" he asked. He straightened, took another few breaths and made himself walk into their room at a normal pace.

"Yes."

Except, it wasn't. He froze just inside the door, dumbstruck by the sight that greeted him.

Holly knelt in the middle of the bed, her small feet tucked up beneath her, her hips cocked at a slight angle so her torso curved in a provocative way. She wasn't showing much, yet, just a subtle rounded tightness of her lower belly – which was on display now, given what she was wearing. New lingerie: emerald green satin bra and panties that emphasized the Old Hollywood hourglass loveliness of her figure, the fullness of her breasts and hips. No stick-shaped magazine model had ever looked so appealing to him. But that was a dim thought, that normal chime of attraction in the back of his mind. Because in this moment, all he could really think about or focus on was the long coil of rope in her hands.

"What the fuck?"

Holly took a deep breath, chest straining at the fitted green satin. She touched one bra strap, brows knitting together. "You don't like it?"

He frowned, gesturing at the rope. "You know that's not what I'm talking about."

She took another breath and glanced down at the coarse hemp in her lap. She traced one of the spirals with her thumbnail, hand trembling. "I keep having nightmares."

"I know. I'm there for them."

"Well...I....." Her hair had been brushed out and softly curled at the ends, and it shone, heavy and brilliant as it fell around her shoulders. "Do you remember, back at the New Years party?"

How was he going to forget that? "Yeah."

"Do you remember, in the dorm room..."

The two of them naked in front of a mirror. It was one of his favorite memories to return to, in quiet boring moments at work.

"...and you said that facing my fears might help." She had to stop and swallow. And then she finally lifted her eyes to his; huge, almost the same shade as her lingerie. "And now I'm not so afraid of mirrors."

With an awful lurch, he realized her intent. "Holly, no—"

"I've been having nightmares about the ropes."

" – absolutely not."

Her lips trembled as she took her next breath, her eyes haunted as they latched onto his. The look on her face would stay with him for months, years, forever. She lifted both hands, the rope held between them, and Michael felt the trembling begin in his calves and move upward, until he was consumed; until the breath rattled in his lungs and his eyelids twitched.

"Michael," she said. "I think...I think you ought to use these on me. I think I ought to face that fear."

Oh God, what was she doing? Was she truly inviting this?

But she wasn't afraid of him, of what he'd do to her, only of her memories. Because this was her Michael, and she trusted him in every way possible. She loved him...sometimes more than the life she carried within her, she was ashamed to admit. Mothers should love their children above all else. But she wasn't a mother yet, and this man was the center of her universe, and the rhythm of her beating heart.

"Tie me up," she said, hating the thready sound of her voice. "Tie me up and touch me, and maybe the nightmares will go away."

His expression made her want to crawl under the covers. And it also made her want to lie him down on the pillows and fetch him a ginger ale, because he looked a lot like he might throw up.

He scrubbed at the back of his neck and stared at his boots a long, silent moment, the energy coming off him cold and unhappy.

"You don't want to." One hand ghosted over the slight protrusion of her belly. She wasn't exactly skinny anymore. She was starting to look pregnant. She –

"I won't do it." His voice was hoarse. His eyes were dark and fathomless when they lifted to meet hers. "I won't *ever* do it. Don't you dare ask me again."

Her breath caught in her throat. "I thought–"

"That if you felt the ropes cutting into you, and you saw it was me on top of you, somehow all that bad shit would go out of your head?" he asked as he walked toward her and dropped onto the edge of the bed like he was exhausted.

She sat up straighter, clenching the rope in her fists. "Well you're the one who gave me the idea."

"No, I never gave you that goddamn idea." But he didn't sound angry. He dropped his head into his hands, elbows braced on his knees, and he looked older than his thirty-eight years. In the early evening light coming through the blinds, Holly could see the little silver hairs sprinkled along his temples.

What was she doing? She was only making the distance between them worse. When Ava had mentioning working things out in the bedroom, she undoubtedly hadn't meant *this*.

Holly set the rope beside her on the duvet and crawled toward him, so she knelt at his side, so she could drape her arm across his tense shoulders and lay her head against the top of his. He sighed deeply and she felt him relax beneath her touch.

"I have nightmares too," he said, quietly, staring down at the carpet, fingers still speared through his hair. "Every night. That I don't get you to the hospital in time. That you're already dead when I pick you up. I dream that I find you tied up in our bed covered in blood, and I chase those bastards as far and as fast as I can, but I never catch them."

She sucked in a breath. "Oh, Michael."

"Sometimes," he said softly, "I dream that I found you when you were still a kid. Before they...And I take you out of there."

Her throat tightened and her eyes burned. She turned her head so her lips were buried in the soft prickliness of his hair. "Michael. Love."

"And I hate that I scare you sometimes. I hate it."

"You don't scare me." She stroked the side of his neck, felt the thundering pulse there. "That's not possible."

His head lifted and turned, so their foreheads touched. His breath was warm across her face, scented with mint, because he'd popped a Tic-Tac before coming home to her. So he had nice breath when he kissed her. Because he wanted her to be comfortable always. Because he loved her.

"Michael," she repeated, her eyes flooding with tears. "What would I do without you?"

"You'd be just fine," he said roughly.

"No."

They sat for a long time, breathing, soaking in the warmth of one another.

Then Michel pulled back, and his gaze went to the length of rope, his eyes hooded, mouth tugged down in a grim frown. He reached for it slowly, curled his hand around it. "I've got a better idea." His eyes flashed up to her face. "You tie me up."

Holly couldn't believe this was happening. If she hadn't heard the rustle of the sheets, smelled the faint whiff of laundry detergent lifting up from them, or seen Michael preparing himself, she would have chalked this up to some strange dream. And not a good one, either. She hadn't intended the evening to take this turn. She'd wanted to exorcise some of her demons, if she could, not turn the tables around on Michael.

Michael was stretched out naked on his back. He was aroused, had been since he'd first shucked his jeans moments ago; apparently, he liked the lingerie after all.

He let his arms fall out toward the edges of the mattress. The undersides were pale in contrast to the golden tan of his shoulders and biceps. A real, working man's tan, and not something he'd cultivated through careful sunbathing.

He lifted his head off the mattress, looked down his body toward her, where she was perched on the edge of the bed. "Tie me up, Hol." It wasn't said with any sort of licentious intent, but his arms flexed as the words left his mouth, and his cock twitched.

Her mouth was dry suddenly. She had to wet her lips to say, "Okay." And then she moved up the bed on her knees.

She was very aware of the way each breath lifted his chest, expanded his ribcage. She heard the air whistling between his clenched teeth as she laid one hand on his wrist and passed the rope gently around it.

"Tight," he instructed, head turning toward her. Tight the way she'd been tied. Tight enough to break the skin, to leave scars.

"No," she said, making a loose knot and stretching the rope toward the bedpost.

"Hol–"

"I'm in charge, and I say no."

This whole scenario was like a dream sequence. It didn't feel like a part of her real life; she'd stepped into a movie; was playing a part in some stage performance that called for her to do these things she'd never envisioned herself doing.

She climbed over him and tied his other wrist to the far bedpost. And then he was her captive, stretched across the bed, waiting and at her mercy.

Holly lifted her hand, hovered it over his chest…

And could do nothing.

Her hand quivered, and then grew blurry as her eyes filled with tears. She didn't want to cry, but her chest was tight and her head was spinning and the sight of her naked husband spread before her should have been sexy, but only felt like the biggest violation of his masculinity.

"Holly."

She blinked the tears away and glanced up at his face. The tenderness in his expression was nearly her undoing.

Softly, sweetly, like he knew exactly what was happening inside her, he said, "Sweetheart, come here and kiss me."

She braced her hands on his pecs and leaned forward, hair falling over her shoulders, to press her lips to his. She closed her eyes and tasted his mouth, pushed the ropes and the old trauma out of her mind. Let the warm smell of his skin and the firmness of his body beneath her swamp her senses. Just the two of them, his chest swelling under her hands, his tongue sliding between her lips. Even though she was the one on top, he had control of the kiss, was working her jaw open wider and taking the inside of her mouth for his own.

She pulled back a fraction to catch her breath, not wanting to put too much distance between them, still wanting her lips to touch his.

59

"What do you wanna do?" he asked her in a low, rough voice that left her pulse throbbing between her legs. "You can do whatever you wanna do to be, baby."

An incoherent sound left her throat. A hard shudder gripped her, left her insides clenching. Whatever she wanted to do. That had never been an option in her old life, in her life before Michael. Her wants, her needs…he was so impossibly good to her.

And she was so very hot and wet for him.

She closed the gap and kissed him again, one leg easing across him, so she straddled his stomach. She slowly let herself relax, until her weight was distributed across his torso. Not much weight, he would have said. She was small. And so when he surged upward against her, leaning into the pressure of her breasts, flexing his abs so the hard ridges rubbed against her sex, she thought he might toss her clear off the bed.

But then he settled, and he kissed her hungrily, his hips flexing the slightest and then releasing, flexing and releasing, as he sought friction between their bodies.

He was very, very turned on, she realized, and he couldn't put his hands on her, because she'd tied him to the damn bed.

The realization was dizzying. She latched onto his shoulders and let his solid hardness anchor her as her lips and tongue accepted the invasion of his kiss.

His body gave another of those great tidal wave movements beneath her, and he grunted against her mouth, breaking the kiss with a ragged sound. "No pressure or anything, but baby, damn, you're gonna have to do something."

"I know, I know." She was, because neither of them had expected this turn of events to prove so incendiary, and he needed some relief from the ache of wanting.

She kissed the side of his throat, the pounding pulse there, the slight salt taste the day had brought out in his skin. Down to the hollow at the base, where she pressed her tongue – and heard the creak of the ropes as he pulled against them.

She started to lift her head. "Are you–"

"Don't stop." A tight, strained voice, nothing Michael-like about it.

The sight of him, his head pressed back into the pillow, the tendons stretched tight along his throat, melted her insides, sent heat pouring through her that vaporized all worry, wonder, and shame. She was doing this to him: popping all the muscles in his arms, pushing him over the edge into a crippling desire that he could only wait out, because she was the one in control.

Holly shifted down his body, leaving a trail of kisses across his chest, the leaping muscles of his stomach. She crawled backward, skimming her lips across as much of him as she could, long, lingering kisses pressed to the soft skin below his navel.

When she wrapped her hand around his cock, his hips surged off the mattress and he cursed between his teeth, all of his body one glistening, straining line of tension.

"I'm sorry," Holly murmured, sliding her hand up his length, passing her thumb over the velvet-soft skin at the head. "Really sorry."

She lowered her head and took him in her mouth. Shallowly, at first. She had no idea if she was any good at this. Before Michael, it had only ever been hands knotted tight in her hair and hammering hips that gagged and choked her and made her sick.

But Michael was always very gentle; he always gritted his teeth and let her move at her own pace, exploring him slowly.

She was slow now not out of uncertainty, but because she was hypnotized by this moment of complete trust on his part. She'd entrusted him with everything she had, and he was doing same.

She sucked at him lightly, just at the head, as if she were kissing his mouth. And when he groaned something incoherent she relaxed her jaw and took him in deeper, her hands holding him steady, massaging him.

As she brought him to release with her hands and mouth, she felt a faint stab of guilt. This was almost like torturing him. But he had volunteered, and the sounds filtering between his clenched teeth were not frightened, tortured sounds. They spoke only of passion and satisfaction and a deeper longing.

He finished, but he didn't calm, and she was glad for it, trailing her fingers up his slippery cock as she straightened, feeling the hot wetness between her legs.

"Do you like the green," she asked, surprised by how breathless she sounded. "Or is naked better?"

"Fuck. *Naked.*"

She fumbled with the clasp of the bra, pushed the panties down her hips and kicked them free. She imagined the way he'd reach for her, if he could, imagined his hands settling on her hips and squeezing in silent encouragement as she straddled his hips, took him in her hand and lowered down onto him, taking him in her body. Didn't just imagine them, but missed them, longed for their weight pushing her down as she lifted and lowered, searching for a rhythm.

She wanted him to cup her breasts and play with her nipples; wanted his strong fingers kneading at the small of her back as she arched and crested.

But he couldn't touch her, and so she touched him.

She leaned forward, smoothing her hands up his chest and back down again. Tickling at his ribs. Digging grooves into his pecs with the tips of her fingers. He was slick with sweat and her palms glided over him. The perspiration was a high sheen in the late afternoon light, painting him shiny and chiseled as a cover model.

Holly worked him slowly, rocking her hips, small movements, savoring the deep, breathtaking pressure of his cock wedged so tightly inside her. She was dizzy; felt drugged. She wanted it to stretch on and on, this sophisticated flirtation with release, holding right on the edge.

She glanced down at her hands, saw the terrible heaving of his chest as he fought for breath. The twitching in his stomach. Saw the deep crimson flush splashed across her own pale skin, across her swaying breasts and the slight curve of her stomach.

She reached down between her parted thighs and touched herself, just above the place where they were joined, right at the aching little place that –

That was when the ropes gave way.

Or, rather, Michael twisted his balled fists out of the insubstantial knots and got loose.

Holly didn't have a chance to be startled. Suddenly his hands were on her, gently touching her despite the violence that quivered under his skin. He gathered her up and rolled her, withdrawing from her so that he could put her on her back and climb over her. Spread her knees, push her legs up. A desperate, ragged sound echoed in his throat as he passed his fingers across her wet entrance and then found her with his cock. One sure thrust and they were together again, and his hands braced on the mattress beside her head as his hips churned.

Holly wrapped her arms around his neck and clung to him.

Yes, this was what they both needed. This was how it was always the best, when he was above her and she was straining to reach him, to press as close to him as she could.

His breath was a hoarse panting in her ear, his face buried in her hair on the pillow as he lost all control and fell to the mercy of the strong flexing of his back. He could do nothing but thrust into her again and again, and she wanted nothing else.

"God," she breathed against the side of his face, turning her head so the rough grain of stubble rasped the tip of her nose. "Michael, *yes*. Please."

And he gave her everything.

There were no words after, only a collapse, their pulses still raging, breathing still ragged. After a long silent spell, Michael reached for her again and she went all too readily, moving onto her hands and knees at his urging, welcoming him into her body in this position.

It was torture in a way she'd never known before. Not pain and punishment, but a lavishing of pleasure, and passion, and the most earnest affection in the most relentless onslaught.

"Thank you," she said, when it was finally over and awareness had returned to her. She smiled softly at him and reached to touch his face with the back of her hand. Roughness of stubble, faint tacky pull of drying sweat. Total relaxation of his jaw because he was exhausted.

It was dark outside now, and the lamps in the room were a soft buttery glow pooling around their bed. They lay on their sides, facing one another, legs interlaced.

His eyes were large and dark, and not narrowed and cynical as they were in the daylight, in the world outside their bedroom. "Not sure we did what you set out to." He almost sounded regretful.

She passed her thumb across his lower lip; the skin was so soft in comparison to the rest of his face. "Thank you for making sex something that I want, and need, and can't do without."

Instead of literal torture.

His arm was heavy with fatigue, but steady as it went around her waist and drew her in even closer. "I think you're probably always going to have nightmares, baby," he said quietly. "I don't know what to do about them."

"You already do so much."

"Not enough, apparently," he said roughly.

She shook her head. "No, you were right the first time. They probably won't ever go away completely. And it was – it was stupid what I tried to do tonight. That...I won't ask something like that again."

He touched his forehead to hers, so his features were blurry with the closeness. "It wouldn't have helped you to relive that. I can't – I won't ever do what they did to you, Hol. I love you too much."

She closed her eyes; her chest filled up to bursting with overwhelming love for him.

"We could get an alarm system," he continued. "I brought you home some brochures. If it would make you feel better, we could have one put it."

She opened her eyes again. "You would want someone monitoring the house even though you…"

Are part of a giant illegal organization.

"If you'd sleep better, I would."

Ava had told her about this. About how even though the club was supposed to come first with all members – and did ninety-nine percent of the time – a man's old lady was sacred, and in his heart, he put her first each and every time.

"No," she said, feeling stronger. "We're safe here, in this house, and in this city. No one's coming after me. I don't want you to do anything that makes *you* less safe."

"Hol–"

"If there's things you won't do, then there's things I won't do too. And I won't put you at risk of going to jail. Ever. For any reason. I need you here with me."

He took a deep breath and let it out through his nose. A peaceful, contented sound. His hand stirred lightly against the small of her back, aimless petting. One corner of his mouth twitched, the tiny Michael-smile that was for her and her alone. "I did like the green."

"Oh, good," she laughed. "I got a dark blue set, too."

"Hmm."

"Maybe you can see it tomorrow."

"Without the ropes, though."

"Yes. No ropes." She snuggled into his chest, completely done in, and yet unable to stop the shiver of anticipation that went down her spine.

Seven
Thing For Bad Boys

Samantha Walton shuffled the papers she'd been reading, tapped them once on the table to line up all the corners, and set them off to the side, in a stack all their own that was separate from the essays she was grading and her own schoolwork. She really hadn't had the time to spare to read a short story just for the sheer fun of it.

Some days, she wondered why she was pushing herself so hard. She had her master's in English. She had a decent job as a part-time professor at UT. Education, income – check. But she was managing to squeeze a second master's degree into her schedule.

Why? Because deep down, she wanted to write novels, not lecture half-asleep college kids.

She'd known from the outset that teaching at the high school level would have been too soul-crushing for her to bear. University level Brit Lit was better: the students more engaged, the workload lighter, the daily grind a little more inspired. And it gave her the flexibility to work on her second grad school endeavor. She could make her own schedule, for the most part, and that did wonders for her creativity.

And her sanity.

She was teaching one summer course – Shakespeare – and taking one summer course – Poetry Writing. Her students had turned in ten-page papers on *Henry IV, Part I* last week, and she needed to finish scoring them with red pen. She also had to write seven poems and print them off for tomorrow's class. She had plenty to keep her busy, but instead, she'd spent the past twenty minutes reading one of Ava Lécuyer's abandoned box projects.

"*Mon Amour.*" *My love* in French. Everything sounded lyrical and twice as poignant in French, and in this case, it was a fitting title, because the story dripped richness and emotion. The story of a young girl having a sexual awakening could have felt overdone or melodramatic, but in Ava's tactful hands had become something literary and sharp-edged.

So growing up in an outlaw motorcycle club gave a girl an advantage in the flair department. Who knew?

Sam resolved to put the story out of her mind and concentrate on her essays. She collected the MLA-formatted sheets in front of her, uncapped her red pen, took another swallow of Earl Grey for courage…

And her mind went back to the subtle French environs of the story. Ava had a thing for dark, brooding, Byronic heroes, and Sam liked that. No doubt, as Ava had written she'd been thinking of Mercy: his long black hair and the way an easy grin could transform so swiftly into something furious and sinister. It was his kindness and cruelty that had inspired Ava in her writing.

Certainly not her brother.

No, why would anyone think of her brother while writing something romantic?

Sam's cheeks grew hot as she sat staring stupidly at her ungraded papers, because while reading *"Mon Amour,"* it hadn't been Mercy that had filled her imagination – it had been Aidan Teague.

She hadn't taken a good long look at the man since high school. She'd spotted him going down the streets in town on his Harley, had glimpsed him in passing at Ava's baby shower, but mostly, his image lived in her memories. All those stupid, schoolgirl memories she couldn't seem to power-sand out of her mind.

He'd never known she existed when she was sitting in the seat directly behind him in algebra. Hers had been the sort of pathetic *She's All That* crush that she'd inwardly scorned. Hoping one day he'd turn around to borrow a pencil, finally take notice of her, and a Disney masterpiece of a teenage love story would unfold from there.

But such a thing had never occurred. His best friend, Kevin – Tango, now – had been polite to her, smiled at her in a sympathetic way, like he'd known she was hopelessly head-over-heels for his friend. But Aidan had never known that she'd looked on him adoringly.

That had been a very long time ago. And she harbored no such feelings now. In truth, she hadn't really thought about Aidan at all, up until she'd met his younger sister in a creative writing course they shared.

Small world.

But even then, she'd had no desire to lay eyes on Ava's over-tattooed, cocksure brother again. But then she'd read this story, and he'd come trampling through her thoughts, graceless and crass as ever.

"Idiot," she muttered to herself, and dropped her eyes to the paper in front of her, yanking her focus back in the right direction.

Papers. Then poems. No more dwelling on stupid bad boys with gorgeous curly dark hair and –

"Argh," she growled through her teeth. "What the *hell?*"

"What the hell what?" a voice said from the other side of the table, and she jerked upright, leaving a big red skidmark from the pen across the paper. Awesome.

So absorbed in her thoughts, she hadn't heard her sister come in the back door. The sister who now stood opposite her, in the process of letting her backpack, gym bag and purse slide off her shoulders like she couldn't be bothered to hold onto them anymore. The straps slithered down her limp arms and all the gear hit the linoleum with a muffled thump. Erin's look was one of the barest interest, like she'd walk off mid-sentence if Sam didn't make this entertaining.

"Nothing," Sam said, attention returning to her paper. "Just talking to myself."

"You do that a lot."

"Hmm."

Erin's chunky-soled sandals clopped across the floor as she went to the cabinet above the sink, pulled down a glass and filled it at the tap.

"Practice go okay?" Sam asked as she scanned the first paragraph of the essay. This poor student had no idea what a thesis statement was.

"They put me on the top of the pyramid," Erin said, voice proud.

"That's great." Also no surprise; Erin was tiny and fine-boned, and flexible as a cat. She made cheerleading look like walking. Breathing. Something natural and easy. Sam's attitudes about cheering notwithstanding, she and her mother had both been delighted to see Erin excel at something – besides attaining boys' phone numbers. The problem was, however, that she didn't seem to like cheering itself any better than the other after-school activities she'd tried, she just liked the attention it earned her.

If nothing else, it would look good on her college apps and it was getting her out of the house and giving her something productive to do this summer.

"Jesse was there," Erin continued, even more proud. "He came to watch me."

Sam lifted her head and turned to regard her sister over her shoulder. Erin stood leaning back against the sink, arms folded over her puffed-out chest, water glass still in one hand. Her flyaway blonde hair was coming loose from her ponytail in a way that looked artist-rendered. After cheer practice, she'd changed into an indecently short black miniskirt and a white tank top that showed her pink bra. She looked twenty-two instead of fifteen. She looked like trouble waiting for the perfect moment to unfold.

"Oh," Sam said, trying not to sound too concerned. When she "started talking like Mom," as Erin put it, Erin tended to run toward sin even faster. "Jesse Irvine?"

"Um, duh. What other Jesse is there?"

Thank small favors for that. "Well, that was…sweet…of him."

Erin tossed her hair with a little smirking smile. "He brought me home."

Sam couldn't keep her mom-ish frown to herself. "I thought Trina's mom was giving you a ride?"

"She was, but then Jesse showed up, so he did."

"I didn't know Jesse had his license."

"Duh."

"Erin, how old is Jesse?"

Erin sipped her water and glanced away, affecting a bored expression. "Eighteen."

"Oh my God!"

"Oh, so what?" Erin rounded on her, scowl dark.

"I thought he was your age!"

"Like I said, so what?"

Sam swallowed the semi-panicked lump in her throat. "Please tell me hasn't graduated yet."

"Back in May."

"Christ."

"OMG, what is the big damn deal?" Erin slammed her glass down on the counter, water slopping out of it.

Sam abandoned her pen, twisting around to fully face her sister. "The big damn deal is that he's a legal adult and you're–"

"Oh no, don't even go there. What, like I'm some dumb kid? Excuse me, but, like, no."

Sometimes, Sam doubted their blood relation. How could they be sisters?

She took a deep, steadying breath. "Boys that old aren't exactly paragons of virtue. If he's pressuring you, or asking you to–"

"Puh-lease, Sam. Jesse likes me. Why do you always have to think the worst of everybody? Like he's trying to, what, rape me or something? He's my boyfriend. You know, *boy*-friend. That thing you've never had."

Sam straightened up in her chair, cheeks growing warm as someone half her age called her out on her love life. "I've had boyfriends."

"Yeah," Erin laughed. "I'm sure things are sooo hot with you and Dick."

"It's Doug."

"Whatever. You don't know shit about boys, Sam, so just butt out." She left the room with a toss of her ponytail for emphasis, leaving all her gear on the floor for someone else to pick up. God knew she wouldn't come back and collect it later.

Sam sighed. She'd never been much of a sister to Erin, but more of a second mother, especially after Dad's passing. She'd been fifteen when Erin was born, and had changed her diapers, bottle-fed her, carried her around when she was colicky. Dad had died two years after that, and even though Mom had never asked it of her, Sam had taken it upon herself to pick up the slack. She'd gone to UT, even though she'd been accepted to UCLA, and she'd worked odd shifts and she'd made sure she was there when her little sister got off the bus in the afternoons. No, there weren't a lot of guys in her past, because she'd been focusing all her energy on working, getting her education, and taking care of her family.

Not that Erin appreciated that.

Not that men did, either. She'd dated casually, and she'd had sex just enough times to need to count it on two hands, and now she had this thing – whatever it was – with fellow professor Doug Schaffer at school. But she hadn't entertained a full-on crush since high school.

Since she'd endured an unrequited girlhood passion for Aidan Teague.

Well fuck him and his motorcycle. She didn't have a thing for bad boys anymore.

And she had papers to grade.

The next day, after class, Sam called Ava and asked if she needed any help arranging furniture or unpacking boxes or anything, really. Ava replied that she was pretty much done at this point, but that she wouldn't say no to lunch, girl talk, and an opinion on paint colors. Sam put down the windows in her outdated battleship of a Chevy and headed for the Lécuyer house with a grateful sigh.

After much internal debate about revealing Jesse Irvine's age to her mother, she'd decided this co-momming thing worked better if they were honest with one another. Mom had been upset – in a concerned way, and not an angry one. And Erin had exploded at the dinner table, yelling at both of them, storming to her room without eating dinner. Sam had rapped on her bedroom door that morning and gotten no answer. So it was safe to assume she was the enemy now. And Mom had been near tears and not sure what to do. "I just wish she could take after you more," she confided. Sam wished that too, even if there wasn't much to recommend about being her.

The hot air coming through the windows eased the AC-generated chill in her muscles, and the loud rumble of the old car vibrated the knot from between her shoulders. It was one of those picturesque, surface-of-the-sun Southern summer days that stirred heat mirages off the pavement and drove kids to the ice cream parlor en masse. It was summertime and it was hot all over the country, but only the South reveled in the magic of that heat. All the café tables at Stella's were full, sunlight glinting off silverware and the smooth plastic lenses of sunglasses. Every loud jacked-up truck in Knoxville seemed to be on the road, sunburned arms of rowdy boys hanging out the open windows, whatever bro-country was most popular blaring from their staticky speakers.

Pure magic.

Ava and Mercy's little white house still needed the outside tackled with fresh paint and shears for the shrubs, but it no longer looked uninhabited and morose. It was starting to look alive, like a sleeping creature peeking out at the world through cracked lids.

Sam parked beside Ava's truck in the drive and let herself in the back door, into the narrow mud room where the washer and dryer had been installed, and where various pairs of boots were lined up beneath the coat rack.

"Ava?"

"In here."

"Your back door was open."

"Only 'cause I knew you were coming. Turn the deadbolt for me, would you?"

She did, and followed her friend's voice into the kitchen. Ava had made cold cut sandwiches and was taking the plates to the table, where fresh bags of chips and frosty cans of Coke waited. Even from a distance, Sam could tell the bread was deli-grade and soft, and her stomach growled.

"I just put Remy down," Ava said as she sat down in front of her lunch and reached for her Coke. "Which means a circus could set up shop in here and he'd still sleep for an hour."

Sam grinned as she pulled out her chair. "You know, if you have another baby, it'll probably be his polar opposite." If she and her sister were anything to go by.

Ava frowned. "Probably. Siblings seem to be at either ends in this family."

Meaning her and Aidan. Damn, she really didn't need to think about Aidan.

And meaning –

"Things haven't been good with the half-brother?" she asked and took a bite of her turkey on sourdough.

Ava shook her head. "He and Merc hate each other. I guess they have their reasons." A shadow passed through her eyes; there was a story there Sam wasn't privy to, and she knew enough about the Lean Dogs not to press. "But the thing that bugs me is they're both trying to pretend they're not related. And, hello, I'm a skeptic, but all they have to do is look at each other. You saw Colin, right? I'm not imagining the resemblance?"

"They could be twins," Sam assured. It had been eerie to see a short-haired, snarky Mercy come into the living room a few days before. "Fraternal, not identical, but yeah, they are for sure brothers."

Ava nodded in agreement. "Between that nose – it's their grandfather's – and that coloring – the grandmother was full-blooded Cherokee – there's just no question. They even move the same way." She shuddered. "And Mercy refuses to accept that they're related."

"It's shocking and awful for him," Sam guessed.

Ava sighed. "He thinks his father was a saint. And by all accounts, the man was a wonderful father. But even wonderful fathers fall weak. Hell – my dad hooked up with a sixteen-year-old for God's sakes."

Sam felt her brows go up, and Ava smiled.

"My mom. He claims he didn't know how young she was."

Sam nodded, swallowing down sandwich, pretending her own mother wouldn't have gone through the roof over the age difference. If Eileen Walton knew that Ava's husband was thirteen years older than her, she would have disapproved of this friendship, whether Sam was thirty-years-old or not.

"I wish," Ava continued, "that he could see this as a positive thing, because he thinks his whole family's dead, and turns out, he has a relative after all. I think it could be really good for him. But he hates Colin."

"Well," Sam said, "there's hate, and then there's *hate*. If Colin did something really awful to him, that's one thing. But if it's just personality clashing, maybe he can get over it."

"Maybe.

"And I have a real hard time imagining anyone doing anything really awful to your husband and living to tell the tale."

Ava snorted. "Yeah."

The sound of a motorcycle engine cut through the afternoon, distant and growing louder. Ava cocked her head, listening as it drew closer. "My brother," she said decisively, and popped a chip into her mouth.

It shouldn't have, but Sam's stomach shriveled into a little ball, her appetite fleeing. She forced herself to swallow the bite of sandwich in her mouth and reached for her Coke, taking a tentative sip. She shouldn't care at all that Aidan was approaching the house. She didn't, in fact. Nope, not at all. Her pulse was *not* knocking against her eardrums, and her palms were *not* suddenly clammy.

As the growl of the Harley grew louder, punching as the bike rolled over the curb into the driveway, Ava stood. "I better go let him in."

Sounds of the bike shutting off. Ava's bare feet on the hardwood. The back door opening.

"Why are you here?" Ava said.

"Dude, can't you just say, 'Good to see you'?" Aidan said.

Boots coming in, door shutting, footfalls returning.

"No, but really," Ava said as brother and sister entered the kitchen.

Sam sent her gaze skittering across the kitchen, fixing it to a white cabinet face across from her. It was an automatic reaction, one she kicked herself for mentally. An old habit from her teen years that it turned out she hadn't shaken – don't stare boldly at the cocky, swaggering, dark-haired outlaw boy with the gorgeous chocolate-colored eyes. Just act cool and natural, and like she didn't know he existed – then ogle him from the corner of her eye when he sat down.

God, I'm pathetic.

She was also thirty now, so she hitched up her shoulders and purposefully turned her face back to the siblings. She wasn't just some girl in Aidan's class these days; she was his sister's friend, and she had every right to be here.

"...borrow his .30-0-6," Aidan was saying. He opened the door of the fridge, leaned in and plucked a beer off the top shelf. As he did so, his wallet chain swung forward, catching sunlight in fast glimmers. His cut had that chafed, weather-beaten look of leather that was used hard, the patches dusty and faded. Sam stole a look at his ass as he was bent forward at the waist, and silently wished he didn't wear his jeans so baggy.

"It's in the safe," Ava said beside him. "I'll go get it."

Aidan twisted the top off his beer and flicked it onto the counter, took a long pull, head tilted back, throat working as he swallowed.

Sam told herself, aggressively, that it didn't matter if thirty looked damn good on the man, she *was not* interested.

"I can get it," he said, wiping his mouth on the back of his hand. "It's in the bedroom closet?"

"First off," Ava said, holding up one finger, "Merc doesn't want anyone knowing the combination to the safe. And two" – second finger – "do you really want to go pawing through my closet?"

"He doesn't want anyone knowing the combination?" Aidan repeated with apparent disbelief. "Don't you know it?"

"It's in my house, so yes, I know it. And it's nothing personal against you – it's just his policy. This is a home thing, not a club thing."

Sam had to bite her lip to keep from laughing. Aidan's expression was a hilarious blend of indignant, wounded, and doubtful. Like he was wondering when the hell his little sister had turned into this adult who was someone's wife and most trusted confidant. By all rights, Aidan's face was one of those severe, laser-cut ones that shouldn't have been capable of much emotion, but that had never been true. He was dramatically expressive, even with those cruel, slanted eyebrows.

"I'm family," he protested. "We're brothers *and brothers.*"

"Just wait here," Ava told him, spinning and leaving the room. Sam thought there was a small pleased curve to Ava's mouth, a private delight in being able to trump all types of brotherhood in this one small instance. It made Sam want to smile too: the women of this club, she was realizing, were the secret beating heart of the organization, in possession of a power over the men that most probably missed, because it was subtle and pretty.

But when Ava was gone, realization crashed over her: She was alone with Aidan. And the last time they'd been alone together, things had gone badly.

Aidan had dropped out of school partway through their senior year. He and Kevin – Tango – both. Not surprising, considering Aidan spent more time in detention than in class, but still, it had seemed sort of extreme in Sam's eyes. Lots of guys hated school and bitched about it, disrupted class and flunked the occasional course. But most didn't just give up. And even fewer dropped out because they'd just been fully patched into their father's motorcycle club and were too busy being an outlaw to bother with studying.

The first week of that senior year, Sam and Aidan had both been held after class by their English teacher, Mr. Murdock. Aidan because he'd thrown a wad of tape across the room and gotten it stuck in Melissa Parkerson's hair; Sam because she'd been accidently placed in regular Lit, when she should have been in AP. Mr. Murdock told them both to wait, and then Mrs. Adams from down the hall had poked her head in the door, breathless and frazzled, and said there were two students fighting in the hall, could Mr. Murdock please come try to assert his "masculine advantage" in breaking the boys up.

"You two sit tight. I'll be back," Mr. Murdock had said, and sprinted from the room.

Then, it was just them.

Sam eased down so she sat on the edge of the desk in the front row, books clasped to her chest, almost protectively. As much as Aidan made her knees weak, left her belly tight with this new adult tension she had no idea what to do with, he spooked her a little too. She had no idea how to act in front of him.

Aidan wasn't allowed to wear his prospect cut at school, but he didn't need it; everything about him screamed renegade. His Levi's were ripped down the front and the hem of the left leg had gotten caught in the top of his boot. A very heavy black boot with spur straps made of chains and ragged laces that cinched them all the way up to mid-calf. He wasn't supposed to wear a wallet chain, but he'd left it on and stuffed it down in his pocket; it was sliding out now, a bright silver snake defying orders as it crawled down onto the teacher's desk he leaned against. He had a new tattoo on his left forearm, and his sleeves were pushed up far enough for her to see the gauze he'd wrapped around it. Another school rule: no visible tats. He was wearing an old Molly Hatchet concert shirt that must have been his father's. It fit him well; he clearly worked out *a lot*. His hair was, as always, spectacular, black-dark under the fluorescent tubes, wildly curly, like a little boy's.

Aidan braced his hands back behind him on Mr. Murdock's desk and exhaled toward the ceiling, like he so didn't have time for all this. "So what'd you do?" he asked, and Sam nearly jumped out of her skin.

"I'm sorry?"

His head tilted toward her…and his gaze was physically heavy against her. She felt her shoulders curl beneath it. "Why's he keeping you after? What'd you do?" He grinned a sudden, startled sort of grin that made him look absolutely evil. And delicious. "You're not fucking the guy, are you?"

74

The crudity of the word, and the shock of the suspicion nearly sent her bolting from the room. "No!" She sat up straight, cheeks bursting into flame. "Of course I'm not!"

His eyes raked over her, to her toes and back, like he could see through her clothes and the books she held tight to her chest. His smile dimmed. "Yeah, guess not." Like he saw her for what she was, when he really looked at her. Like she was plain and ordinary and not-hot, and why the hell would a teacher risk getting fired for the sake of being with her? Like she was just another faceless nerd beneath his notice.

Shame was like a sword going through her, rivaled only by the piercing embarrassment.

"I didn't do anything," she said, because it hurt too badly to accept his scorn. "I'm in the wrong class. I'm supposed to be in AP, not in here." *With your stupid ass,* she added silently.

He snorted and turned away, expression bored again. "Sounds about right."

Why, oh why, she wondered, did she have to have the most terrible crush on this smarmy asshole?

She didn't understand his insistence on being a dick. And doing stupid things in class that got him in trouble. Didn't real outlaws have better things to do than pull pranks?

"Why'd you do it?" she asked, voice coming out sharper than she'd intended.

"Do what?"

"Throw the tape. Why'd you do that?"

He shrugged and stared at the classroom door. "Melissa's a bitch."

"I thought you dated her."

"Yeah. 'Date.' If that's what you wanna call it." He smirked and then sobered again. "She's still a bitch."

The heat in her face was going to melt her brain, she decided. Date, if that's what she wanted to call it. So he'd slept with her. How many of their classmates had he been with, she wondered. Everyone but her?

"She wouldn't be a bitch to you," she said, before she could stop herself.

"Yeah right."

Sam shook her head, chasing the memory away. That had been so long ago, and it shouldn't hold any bearing on the here and now. Now they were both adults, and they were in his sister's kitchen, and they'd both doubtless moved beyond their high school selves.

Aidan was drinking his beer, leaning back against the kitchen sink, his pose eerily identical to that of their classroom conversation years ago. Still the chain, and the boots, and the dark hair, plus the edge in his dark eyes. All of it enhanced by time.

He glanced over in a cursory way, just a flicker of a glance.

Sam pushed her plate away and wrapped her hand around her Coke can to ensure it didn't look wobbly and betray her. Stupid hand.

Then Aidan glanced again, really looked at her, and if anything, he'd only gotten better at undressing people with his eyes. He studied her a moment; she felt him notice the thick dirty blonde braid pulled over her shoulder, her casual, loose white tank top, her glasses, her mouth, her breasts. Then he smiled.

Holy shit. That smile.

"Hey."

"Hi," she returned, grateful she managed not to squirm in her seat.

His smile widened, and took on an easy, flirtatious quality that was truly swoon-worthy. If she were the sort of girl who swooned, which she wasn't. "Ava didn't say she had a hot friend. I feel like she's been holding out on me."

She took a small, insubstantial breath, but was proud of the way her voice was steady. "Well, there's Leah and Holly."

He rolled his eyes. "Leah might as well be my sister. And Holly's...fucked up and pregnant and married, so...yeah." The grin came back. "But then there's you."

What the hell did she say to that? "Thank you...?" She couldn't quite come to grips with the fact that this guy, of all guys, was calling her hot and flirting with her. It just didn't seem possible.

"Wait, you were at her baby shower, weren't you?" he asked.

"Yes. And I've been helping with the unpacking."

He nodded, still smiling. "Right." He pushed off the counter, stepped closer to the table. "I'm Aidan, by the way..."

Oh, God.

"...I know she probably talks a buncha shit about me..."

He was introducing himself to her.

"...but it's only half true."

Because he didn't remember her at all.

Still grinning like a demon, he said, "So what's your name?"

All the nervous jitters left her in a flood. A flood of shame and anger and embarrassment, because for a little bit there, she'd lost her mind, and allowed herself to feel giddy as a teenager about the fact that he was coming on to her.

In a flat voice, she said, "Sam. Sam Walton."

Still, he didn't remember. "Alright, Sam, I gotta know how you ended up friends with my totally lame sister."

She resisted the urge to growl at him. "I met her at school. We have class together. Where else would us totally lame writing nerds hang out?"

That pushed him off his game a little. "Ah…so you're…into books and stuff too?"

"Yes. Books. And stuff."

"Well…hey, that's cool…" Like he was giving her permission to be a nerd. Like it was somewhat acceptable that she be uncool.

"Look," she snapped, "I'm going to put you out of your misery here, Teague. We've met before. We went to high school together. You have spoken to me before. But clearly, you don't remember that, because clearly, I was never up to the level of your social strata, and completely beneath your notice. You're about twelve years too late to put the moves on me, you jackass."

The look of total shock on his handsome face was gratifying.

"Whoa," Ava said as she stepped back into the room, a rifle in a zippered case propped on one shoulder. "Should I give this to you?" she asked Sam. "You look like you want to put a round through him, and I could get on board with that."

Aidan stood frozen, speechless.

"No, it's okay," Sam said, staring him down, "I think he feels stupid enough without the bullet."

"Okaaaay." Ava stepped forward, handed her brother the gun and he took it with wooden, clumsy hands. "There you go. Anything else?"

He shook his head slowly, blinking a lot as he turned his head and refocused on his sister. He looked like he'd been in a car accident. "Nah. This is it."

"Okay. Have a safe ride back. Give Mercy a kiss for me."

" 'Kay," he said, not even acknowledging her request with so much as a frown. He glanced back over his shoulder at Sam once before heading to the back door.

Ava followed him, locking the door, and then returned, eyebrows raised. "What was that about?"

The bike started up in the driveway, an angry snarl.

"I think…I think he was hitting on me. Because he didn't remember who I was."

Ava snorted. "What an asshole."

"Yeah."

Ava sat down again. "Oh, so, like I was saying…" She reached for her sandwich.

Sam nodded. She forced food into her mouth, and she hoped her answers were appropriate, because she wasn't thinking about the Mercy/Colin problem at all. Her mind had gone out the back door with Ava's brother, and she couldn't believe how badly it still hurt to be invisible.

Eight
Sex Ed

Lunch. All he wanted was a sandwich. There ought to be some deli ham and Swiss in the clubhouse fridge. Tango had food on the brain as he walked into the blessedly cool common room.

And he pulled up short when he saw what was happening at one of the round dining tables.

Jasmine was having an afternoon gin and tonic – normal – and she was all done up for a party – also usual. Denim miniskirt, tight western shirt that flashed lots of cleavage, hair in big barrel curls, makeup ready for a nightclub.

But she wasn't alone. A brunette girl Tango had never met before sat beside the Lean Bitch, hands wrapped around a beer bottle, her smile small and nervous as she listened to what Jasmine was saying.

Jasmine noticed him and got to her feet. "Baby boy!" she greeted excitedly, beaming. "Come here. I want you to meet someone."

Overcome by a sudden cold dread, he stepped forward, lifting his arm as Jazz slid beneath it and hugged him around the wait, kissed the side of his neck. She smelled – ha – like jasmine, her usual perfume.

"What's going on?"

Jasmine wiggled against him, stood up on her toes, beamed, and made a grand gesture toward the brunette. "Tango, this is Bridget."

The girl managed to duck her head while making eye contact, and gave him a little wave. "Hi."

"Yeah…um, hi," he said, and turned to look at the woman pressed against him. "What's going on?"

She kept smiling. "You know how I keep saying you need to find you a nice girl? Well, I found you one. I set up an online dating profile for you."

"You did *what*?"

"Ratchet let me use his computer. I can show you all of it later. But anyway," she said firmly when he started to protest, "that's how I met Bridget, and she wanted to meet you, so…" She gestured toward the girl again, brows waggling. "What you doin' for lunch, baby?"

"Is…is this okay? Is it good for you?"

Midafternoon sunlight beamed in through the high, frosted window above the bed, like a spotlight on the girl in the middle of the hazy dorm room. The shy brunette – shit, he couldn't remember her name – had her shirt off, sporting a lacy pale pink bra and a truly impressive set of breasts hefted up in its cups. Her denim skirt was bundled up to her waist and she was naked beneath, her thighs spread wide across his hips, his condom-covered cock rooted deep in her sex. She was holding very still, an uncertain blush coloring her cheeks, her hands pressed to the bare flat of his belly. She was so aroused she was trembling – and there was no doubting the wetness between her legs – but she was hesitant and almost cringing. Up for the sex, but not sure where to go from here.

God, kill him now.

Technically, he wanted this. His cock had come to full attention under her hand. And technically, he'd been willing enough as he'd undressed and pulled her up to straddle him. But this wasn't the sort of thing that was going to push memories back, override his brain and bring him any sort of release.

"It's fine," he said through his teeth.

But it wasn't. He never should have let Jasmine talk him into this.

As if she were reading his mind from the chair against the wall, Jasmine stabbed out her cigarette in the nightstand ashtray and got to her feet, moving to stand beside the bed.

"You've got to relax, baby," she said, and she was talking to the girl, a hand settling on the brunette's shoulder, squeezing lightly.

The girl turned her head a fraction, eyes wide with alarm as she stared at the groupie.

"Here." Jasmine stepped closer. "You've gotta let yourself go." She tucked the girl's hair back behind her ear, trailed her forefinger along the delicate jaw afterward.

The girl pulled in a shivery breath.

"I'll help you," Jasmine declared, and she climbed onto the bed, straddling his legs and scooting up until her front pressed against the girl's back. Until they were fitted together like clothes on skin.

The brunette jumped a little as Jasmine's hands settled on her hips.

"Shh," the groupie murmured. "Let's find a rhythm. Here. Up, and back, up, and back." She leaned forward and back herself, urging subtle movements of the girl's hips with her hands, until both of them were slow-dancing at the same sultry pace, hips to hips, breasts to back.

The brunette's breathing picked up. Her chest lifted, pink bra straining.

"Good girl," Jasmine praised. Her hands slid forward, pressing down low on the girl's belly, urging her to bear to down, to grind side-to-side. "Just like that." She shifted a little herself, and Tango knew she was aroused, the way her pelvis tilted forward.

The movement was helping, tightening him up, making him squirm just a little.

Jasmine's hands drew slowly up the girl's sides, skimmed forward, closed over the lacy bra cups. "Nice," she whispered. "Real?"

The girl's head half-turned, eyelids drooping. "Yeah," she whispered back.

Jasmine's talented thumbs found the little knobs of the girl's nipples and traced them through the lace. Flicking back and forth. Pressing. She leaned in even tighter.

Then her hands slid around to the girl's back. There was a soft *clip* sound, and then the pink bra was loosening, the straps sliding down her arms.

"There," Jasmine purred. "Let's get comfy." She urged the girl's arms to leave first one strap and then the other, then tossed the bra aside. The full, pink-tipped breasts were spectacular. Drawn up tight, the nipples peaked in a way that looked painful.

Jasmine reached around the girl's front and took the heavy breasts in her hands, her black fingernails stark against the pale skin. She kneaded them with sure movements, changing their shapes as she lifted them.

The girl gasped.

"Yeah," Jasmine said. "You like that?"

"Oh…" the girl said, and her chest surged, breasts thrusting into the hands that petted them.

Jasmine clutched on tight, and urged the girl to lean back against her, squeezing.

The brunette complied, letting her weight rest against the head Lean Bitch, her hips bucking and swiveling in helpless reaction. Her eyes fluttered shut, and her lips parted on a wordless sound. She panted. Her hands lifted, and she pressed them to the backs of Jasmine's hands, encouraging, holding on for dear life as she ground against him.

Over the girl's shoulder, Jasmine smiled at him, her grin absolutely wicked as she pinched the girl's nipples. Then she turned her head to the side and ran her tongue up the girl's throat.

The girl let out a strangled moan and her sex clamped tight around his cock. Grabbing him and releasing, grabbing him and releasing as she came. Her face flushed a pretty crimson and her hips kicked.

By all rights, Tango should have been arched beneath the two of them like a bowstring, his own release tackling him.

But girl-on-girl had never really been his thing.

Timid strangers were yet less his thing.

The girl was coming back down, breathing in dreamy sighs, her eyes fluttering open as her hips stopped gyrating.

"Lie down, baby," Jasmine said, urging her off of Tango and onto the bed beside him. She collapsed, boneless. Her lashes flickered as exhaustion swamped her.

Jasmine was still straddling him, and she scooted forward, peeling the glistening condom off his still very hard cock. "Baby boy," she scolded, wrapping her expert hand around his length. "You can do soooo much better than that." Mock censure in her frown, delight sparking in her eyes.

His legs flexed, heels digging into the mattress as he fought the urge to lift into her sure, strong touch. "Sorry. Guess I'm not much into three-ways."

Her frown threatened to turn into a grin. "Try again. I know, straight from the horse's mouth, that Misty broke you and Aidan in together when y'all were kids."

Only partially true. Yes, the then-famed Misty had taken it upon herself to deflower the two of them when they were sixteen. And yeah, he and Aidan had both been in that dorm room with her. But only Aidan had been a first-timer. Tango had lost his virgin status fully at age twelve. And before that – well, it all depended on one's definition of sex.

"What I want to know…" Jasmine gripped him tight and leaned forward at the waist, bringing their faces closer, her hair swinging, giving him a look down her shirt to show off her lack of bra. "Is if you boys ever still do that sort of thing." The gleam in her eyes was enough to leave him twitching in her hand.

He knew Jasmine, and he knew this wasn't an idle question.

"Someone you know interested?" he teased.

She dampened her lips. "Yeah."

"I could ask Aidan…"

"God," she breathed. And then she was a flurry of movement. Shoving up her own denim miniskirt. Tearing open the strained buttons of her shirt. Fishing a condom from the nightstand, ripping open the foil and rolling it onto him with lightning precision. Mounting him. Guiding him to her entrance and taking him inside as she sank low, her thighs clenched tight.

She reached for his hands and urged them inside her open shirt, pressing them to the manufactured fullness of her tan breasts.

He cupped her in his palms and squeezed. Lifted his hips and drove hard inside her as she started to move.

"Ask him," she said, voice breathless with arousal. "Oh, please, baby, ask him."

"Okay," he said through his teeth. And then speech wasn't possible, because this was the frenzied, almost violent fucking he'd needed.

The girl at his side stirred. He saw her hand settle on his chest, then move lower, gliding over the knotted, working muscles in his abdomen as his thrusts lifted his pelvis. The hand reached Jasmine's knee and slid up the other woman's thigh.

A delighted sound left Jasmine's throat and she bore down on him hard, her nails scoring his stomach.

Okay, Tango thought, as the brunette's hand slipped up under Jasmine's skirt, maybe girl-on-girl wasn't his least favorite thing in the world...

It was two days later that curiosity finally got the best of him and he looked up his own online dating profile. Jasmine had given him the username and password she'd used, and he just happened to be the only one in the clubhouse at the moment. And Ratchet's laptop just happened to be on, open, and abandoned. The web browser was even pulled up, the Google search bar waiting with cursor at the ready.

He checked over his shoulder to make sure he was truly alone, then threw himself down into the chair. "Oh, fuck me." His fingers were nervous on the keys, and he had to backspace and retype the web address three times before he got it right.

Shit, shit, shit, he thought as he opened up the page and logged on.

One-percenters didn't have online dating profiles. They didn't search out women on the internet. They didn't let goddamn *groupies* find dates for them.

Just humoring Jasmine, he reasoned. Because God knew he didn't need another semi-awkward, semi-hot afternoon like he'd had a couple days ago. He wasn't interested in making that a regular thing.

He let out a slow, defeated breath through his teeth and scanned the profile. Jasmine had taken a picture of him while he slept on the clubhouse sofa. His head was turned to the side, one arm raised up over his head. He was frowning in his sleep, brows drawn together, making him look very serious. The seven little hoops marching down the lobe of his ear and the tat snaking out of the neck of his shirt were very visible.

There was a second photo, a half-blurred cellphone shot from a distance. Jasmine had cropped his brothers out of the picture, so it was just a narrow image of him laughing at something Mercy had said. At least he was smiling. But then again, when he smiled, all the metal and funky hair sort of faded into the background, and made the fine-boned, almost-feminine lines of his face more noticeable.

He frowned and saw his dim reflection in the computer screen. No matter how many tats or piercings or inches of shaved head, he would always be, beneath it all, the very pretty boy Carla had bought from Frederick. The boy who…

Nope, not going there.

There was an inbox up in the left corner of the screen, where other members of the site had sent him messages, and he had four. Three were from women: two normal girls looking to take a walk on the wild side, and one truly scary Goth chick he X'd out of quick.

And then there was the fourth.

No picture, just a screen name: Lord Byron. A man.

The message read: *My, I thought all you bad boys were drowning in pussy. God, I despise that word. It's vile. Message me. We ought to catch up.*

"Ian," he murmured, shoulders deflating. Only Ian Byron could have affected such a complete transformation of his life. And only he would have the resources and energy necessary to find this profile and reach out through it.

Don't do it, a voice in the back of Tango's head urged. He should delete this entire account, tell Jasmine to fuck off, and pretend none of this had ever happened.

But his hands were gliding over the keys.

No!

The inner voice railed against a body that seemed to move of its own accord, fingers typing a message and sending it.

What are you doing, Ian?

The response came within minutes. *Talking to an old friend. Is that a crime?*

Tango could picture the asshole's smug look, the way self-satisfaction put his austere features to their best use. He was, after all,

84

from a prestigious London bloodline. He'd never been an English street rat, no matter how he'd been treated. Breeding was evident in everything he'd ever done, even when he was…

Probably, he typed back. *Isn't it bad enough you're trying to take down my club? You gotta cyberstalk me too?*

Not taking down, and not stalking, Ian typed back. *Can't we talk, Kev? Not as adversaries, but as the friends we truly were.*

Tango screwed his eyes shut tight. Unbidden, his mental picture of Ian as he was now – flashy suit, tidy slicked-back hair, manicured hands and shiny shoes – was replaced with an old image, one of Ian at seventeen, all arms and legs and lithe grace, eyes ringed in the black liner Carla had painted them with to "attract the customers."

Another message from Ian: *Come have lunch with me. No club, no business. Just you and me.*

That was a terrible idea.

But he could almost hear the guy's voice, the gentleness and pleading in it that had nothing to do with the composed mask he'd shown the day the Dogs had entered his office.

Tell you what, Ian typed. *I have some business to attend in Knoxville. Afterward, I'll be at the steakhouse at three o'clock. Give the hostess my name and she'll show you to my table. If you feel like joining me.*

"Yeah right," Tango muttered, closing the web browser and leaning back in the chair.

But there was a voice in the back of his head reminding him that he'd never had much of a backbone.

He shouldn't be doing this. He should be as far away from this as was humanly possible. But here he stood on the sidewalk, staring up at the sign of one of the most well-known high-end steakhouse franchises. He'd never been in this place. He'd never been anywhere remotely like this place. He didn't belong here, in his baggy jeans and scuffed boots, with his half-buzzed, half-spiked hair and all the bright rings in his ears. McDonald's was fancy for the likes of him. He wasn't fit to be a busboy in a restaurant of this quality.

And yet here he stood. Like a fucking idiot.

With a sigh, he pulled open the door and let himself inside.

There was an airlock that led him to a second pair of doors, these wood and inlaid with frosted glass. Beyond them, the smell of buttered, perfectly cooked steaks curled around his empty stomach and reminded him that he was starving, but too sick at the idea of this meeting to eat anything.

His throat tightened as he crossed the patterned carpet to the hostess station. The place was making a polite go at English library: dark paneled walls, hunt prints, wall sconces, heavy ceiling beams and linen-draped tables studded with glasses and tented napkins, awaiting patrons in the manufactured low light. Elegant, simple, tasteful. Nothing like him.

The hostess glanced up from her podium and gave an obvious start. She was young, her hair pulled back in a tight bun, her uniform crisp and new-looking. She clearly wasn't used to patrons looking like drummers from failing garage bands, and her mouth worked soundlessly a moment before she stammered, "G-good afternoon. Welcome to Ruth—"

"I'm meeting someone," he said, to spare her further awkwardness. "Mr. Byron. He should have reservations."

She consulted her list, cheeks pinking, then nodded. "Yes. Mr. Byron said to expect someone who…" She glanced back up at him and thought better of whatever description Ian had given her. "Come with me, please."

He followed her down the long narrow dining room, thinking, of course Ian was somewhere in the back, out of the fray. Just on the other side of a decorative panel-wrapped pillar, Ian had a table for two beside the shaded window, a view of the sidewalk that was one-way – no pedestrians could see in, but the filtered sunlight struck his marble face in glorious soft relief.

The man who had established himself as Shaman in Tennessee was cut straight from some European men's fashion magazine. He had picked a gray suit that fitted him tightly, accentuating his tall slenderness, rather than hiding it, daring anyone to find fault with his lean, dancer physique. His shirt was a pale green that picked up the darker filaments in his pale eyes, and his hair was, as Tango had seen it a few months before, slicked back off his face, behind his ears, and falling in a shiny auburn sheet past his shoulders. His face showed his breeding: cheekbones that could cut glass, narrow, high-ridged nose. And the way he stared out the window was just shy of casual, betraying the wealth of hurt beneath the surface. He was British, though, and from a good family – though they probably had no idea he was still alive – and he wasn't going to wallow in what had happened. He was going to press elegantly forward toward what was to come. Stiff upper lip and all that.

His head turned as the hostess dropped the menu on the table with a murmured word and disappeared.

"Thank you," Ian said to the departing employee, but his eyes were on Tango, with unnerving intensity. Eyes that were neither blue nor green, but some color between. An expression that, despite its intense energy, had some indefinable feminine quality to it. He'd always had that; it had been one of the reasons he had been so popular with Carla's customers. It was one of the reasons –

Not going there.

He stood like a silent moron behind the chair opposite Ian, tongue glued to the roof of his mouth. He had nothing to say because this was stupid, and he shouldn't be here in the first place.

Ian gave him a partial smile. "You look well."

"I look like shit." He started to turn. "And I shouldn't be here."

"Sit down, Kevin." It was said with gentle authority. "God knows you could use a good meal, and you didn't walk all the way in here just to tell me off and leave."

Tango ground his molars together. No, he hadn't come here just to leave. He'd been hoping the whole ride over that he'd find the balls to turn back around and head for the clubhouse.

But when had he ever had the balls for anything? He was a follower. A friend. A wingman, and a sidekick. He didn't make decisions that were his own. Never had.

Cursing inwardly, he dragged out the chair and threw himself in it. "This is fucked up," he muttered. "If my prez knew…"

"Will you tell him? Ghost. Will you tell him you met with me today?" Slight tilt to his head, penetrating X-ray stare.

Tango had to look away. "What do you think?"

There was a smile in Ian's voice. A gentle smile, like one a parent would give to a child. "I think this has nothing to do with your president, and I don't think he has any right to know about it. You're your own man now, Kevin. You don't need anyone's permission to meet with me."

He snorted. "The boss man wouldn't agree with that."

"Why not?"

"You know how clubs work, don't gimme that bullshit."

Ian made a soft, contemplative sound in the back of his throat. A sound Tango knew well, from all those years of captivity together. "I think," he said, in that crisp accent he should have by all rights dropped during his time in America, "that for the most part, your president sees you as a solider in his army. Because yes, I do know how clubs work, and you can take all the votes you want, but at the end of the day, your president is your king, your general, your bloody Napoleon, and he dictates to you, because it's all about the club for him, and not the individuals in it."

"That's not true." Tango whipped his head around, sent a vicious glare toward the Englishman. In his mind he saw himself at seventeen, sobbing hard enough to pull muscles, arching beneath the onslaught of withdrawal as the heroin left his system. Aidan had been there, but Ghost had been there too. He'd put his callused hand on top of Tango's head and said, "Easy, son. Ride it out. We're right here. You just ride it out." The man was an unforgiving president…but as a father figure, he'd never looked on Tango with the scorn and contempt he'd always expected. He'd never given a damn about the things Tango had done in his previous life.

His life that involved Ian Byron.

Ian lifted his brows. "Isn't it, though? Why else would he protest against this?" Elegant gesture of long fingers to the two of them seated across from one another. "Why would he protest two friends meeting for lunch if not for his club?"

Tango braced his elbows on the table and dropped his face into his hands. "Fuck you."

Soft, cultured laughter. "Oh, that would be lovely."

"Shut up."

"I'm worried about you, Kev. You look unhappy, and that upsets me."

His chest tightened, some nameless emotion cranking his hands into claws against the sides of his face. "You have an empire now," he said quietly. "Why give a shit about me?"

"Because I always did." Gentle, kind voice. "You know that. I had a plan. You know that if they hadn't pulled you out of there I would have—"

"You didn't have shit."

"I did!" Ian insisted. "And obviously it worked, because as you just said, I have an empire."

Tango gapped his fingers and looked at the man's face.

"I got out, Kevin. I got the hell out of there, and look at me. Look at what I have." A quieting of his face, as he leaned back in his chair. He gestured to the shaded window. "See him, out there?"

There was a brick wall of a man on the sidewalk, dressed all in black, looking like nothing anyone wanted to mess with.

Ian had regained his poise. "That's George. Dumb as a bag of hammers, but let anyone get too close to me, and he'll tear windpipes out. He's loyal." His eyes cut over to Tango. "He's respectful." Sharp, cutting smile, flashing straight white teeth. His parents had been wealthy enough Londoners to get him braces. So his teeth would be flawless when he was stolen from his bed at thirteen. "Can you imagine? Me, the nine o'clock special with loyal, respectful employees who'd kill for me?"

He sat forward again, starling Tango. "You could have that too, you know. You don't have to be a solider in someone else's war."

Suddenly, Tango was exhausted. "I'm not doing this." He started to push his chair back, and a waitress materialized at the side of their table.

"Are you ready to order?"

"I am." Ian flicked a questioning look across the table. "Come on. My treat. You know you're hungry."

He was. He was always hungry. He hadn't checked the menu, but Tango ordered a New York strip, medium-rare, baked potato on the side.

"Anything to drink?" the waitress asked.

"Um…"

There was a small bottle of red wine on the table, and Ian tapped it with one long forefinger. "You're not afraid to admit you like it, are you?"

"Nah. I'm good," he told the waitress sourly, and she whisked away.

With a quiet, pleased smile, Ian turned over the second wine glass and filled it with a deft tilt of the bottle. "I thought maybe you'd lost a taste for it, all that beer you must drink."

Tango reached for the glass and took a slow sip, the oily warmth of the merlot coating his tongue and bringing up a hundred half-buried memories. He set it down with a jolt. The reasons he didn't drink wine anymore had nothing to do with the taste.

"You don't like it?"

"I don't like wherever this is heading."

"And where do you think that is?"

"Goddamn it!" He slapped the edge of the table hard enough for the silverware to jump. The nearest table was about fifteen feet away, but the lunching couple glanced over, eyes wide with alarm.

Tango lowered his voice to an angry hiss. "Stop playing games with me. Stop trying to act all mysterious and villainous. You're not Lex Luthor, you asshole, so knock it the fuck off. Why did you ask me here? Huh? Why the hell?"

Ian sipped his wine, eyes growing distant as he pulled back within himself. He scrutinized him a long moment, swished the wine around in his mouth, lowered the glass slowly. Then he swallowed and sat forward with a little lurch, all the old remembered vibrancy coming back to his face, glowing from the inside out with all the raging, angry passion he'd had as a teenager.

"Because it's lonely," he said in a low, intense voice that wouldn't carry beyond the edge of their table. "At first, getting out, climbing up on top of the pile, creating a whole new identity for yourself – it's exhilarating. It's…" His expression was almost dreamy a moment, before the passion returned. "It's indescribable, really, to know that you have achieved something that the ones who hurt you could only lust after. But then…then it turns lonely.

"When I saw you on that dating site, I realized something. You're lonely, too, Kevin."

Tango didn't ask him how he'd mined that profile out of the vast recesses of the Web. Men like Ian had ways of finding things. Instead, he said, "That was just something one of the girls did. It was stupid. It doesn't mean anything."

"But you are, aren't you?"

"What?"

"Lonely."

"No." But he had to look away as he said it, because it was a lie. He wasn't bitterly lonely, not crippled by it. But he didn't share Aidan's zeal for anonymous sex and half-drunken revelry. He was at all the parties, and he'd crammed his share of dollar bills into strippers' thongs, but that didn't reward him in any way. Internally. Internally, there was a sort of aching melancholy that he'd learned to live with as a boy.

Ian was studying him with outward sympathy, the lean pen strokes of his face softened marginally. "I know that, for you, the club was the best way to get free of Carla–"

"I really wish you wouldn't say her name."

" – but I don't think it's really your place. I don't think it's where you belong."

They're my people, he ought to say. *My brothers. Their old ladies are my sisters and their children are my nieces and nephews. We are a family, and that's something you'll never understand because before they lost you, your parents probably didn't even love you.*

Neither had his parents, but he'd found what they'd never given to him in the Teagues, and in the rest of the club.

But instead, he swallowed and said, only half-mockingly, "Where do I belong, then?"

"I don't know. But I'd like to give you the opportunity to find out."

Tango bowed up, hands curled against the edge of the table. "If you think you can turn me against my club—"

"This has *nothing* to do with the club, Kevin." The passion, the coldness, the control and the power all coalesced into the mask of a king on Ian's face. It was terrifying. The boy that he'd been, the boy who had known Tango better than anyone else, had become this noble, platinum-coated monarch, like something straight from Shakespeare's stage. "This is about me telling you that if you are unhappy, and you want to start all over, I will help you do whatever you want. Because you saved my life, and for the affection I bear for you, I will do *anything* to help you. Say the word, and I can change your life."

Nine
Not Cool, Bro

In the years after her violent miscarriage, Ava had wondered what her life would have looked like had the baby not been killed in the womb. If she'd been on the cusp of her eighteenth birthday when her first child was born. She might still have been able to go to college – hell, she was going to grad school now with a baby – and for sure Mercy would have proposed. Would her life have been somehow more magical? No, but she grieved for that lift she'd lost anyway. She didn't wish she'd been a mother at seventeen. She wished the life she'd created with the man she loved most had had its chance to come into the world.

That sting of bitterness was eased in moments like these. Moments when her Remy was a solid, contented bundle in her arms as he nursed from her, the delicate soft curve of his skull cradled in her palm. Everything about him fascinated her. The downy skin of his rounded cheeks. The dark spiky fans of his lashes. The tiny, perfect fingers and toes, and the way they curled as he slept.

No advice, no motherhood manual could have prepared her for this: the way she would be enraptured.

"Done?" she asked as Remy pulled back, and she shifted him gently onto her shoulder, rubbed his back until she felt his ribs expand with a burp. "That's better, isn't it? There we go."

She rose from the sofa and paced slowly down the hall, rocking her upper body in the slight way that always sent him off to sleep. By the time she'd reached the nursery, his eyelids were heavy.

"You take a nap, Big Man." He was no small weight as she leaned over the crib rail and lowered him to the sheets. "And I'll see you in an hour."

She waited, lingering with arms draped over the rail, until his breathing had evened and she was sure he was asleep, then she tiptoed barefoot from the room, leaving the door ajar, straightening her bra and shirt so she was covered.

Mercy had asked her more than once if she was going stir-crazy being at home this much. She wasn't taking summer classes, having needed the semester off to give birth and spend time with Remy. She worked part-time at Dartmoor when she could, but it wasn't a regular gig. Was she bored? He'd wanted to know. Was she feeling locked up? He hadn't asked if she felt like her life was slipping away, but that had been heavily implied by the notch between his black eyebrows.

The poor man had no idea. She was working toward her Creative Writing masters, was writing fiction in her downtime, was married to the man she loved more than life itself and was dreading the day she had to leave Remy with someone while she went to class.

"Stir-crazy" just wasn't part of her vocabulary these days.

In fact, she was pretty sure she'd won the lottery.

The TV was murmuring to itself – a home reno show on in the background to provide white noise. She didn't want Remy requiring absolute silence in order to sleep.

Sunlight fell through the naked windows – they really needed drapes or blinds or something – and lit on the polished floor, the dust-free coffee table. Clean as a whistle around here, and virtually all the unpacking was done. With a satisfied sigh, Ava headed toward the kitchen. She'd grab a snack and boot up her computer, make a little headway on the story she was –

She saw the tall shadow on the other side of the window before the doorbell tolled through the house. She jerked, hand jumping up to cover her startled heart.

A face pressed itself close to the glass and she recognized Colin.

Her pulse changed gears, driving hard in anger now instead of fear. She was in a full-on, super-feminine huff by the time she answered the door. She wedged her body into the gap, refusing to just invite him in. "What are you doing here, Colin?"

"Well, how's that for hospitality?" he asked with a laugh. "You know, you're in the South, darlin'. Aren't ya s'posed to be bringing me a cold glass of tea?"

"A cold glass of what-the-fuck-are-you-doing-here."

His brows went up in an expression of dramatic mock-offense. "Jesus Christ, you're touchy today. Is it–" he leaned in and winked - "your *special time* or something?"

She drew herself up straighter. "You mess with my man, you mess with me, simple as that," she said flatly. "So I repeat: What do you want?"

"Are all you biker women this way?"

"Pretty much."

Some of the humor left him. "Can I come in?"

"What for?"

He sighed. "To wait on your husband to get home."

"You could have done that at the shop."

"I wanted to talk to him here." He shoved his hands in his pockets, titled his head to the side and gave her a look that was much too much like one of Mercy's more charming, boyish glances. His didn't have that disarming honesty, but it was close. "May I please come inside, Ava?" he asked, his accent thinning on purpose, as he said her name with respect that, if fake, was convincing. "I keep trying to hash things out with Felix and we can't seem to get anywhere. I want to finish this, once and for all."

"If you're hoping to change his mind, I've got a news flash for you: not gonna happen. But you can come in, yeah," she relented, stepping back and clearing the way for him to enter. "The baby's asleep, so keep it down."

He nodded, and remembered to take his boots off, shucking them just inside the door.

Ava watched him as she turned the deadbolt, the way his eyes took in the improvements, the orderliness, the lack of liquor boxes and Rubbermaid tubs. The walls needed paint, and the light fixtures needed updating, but it looked like a home now, and not a transitional space.

"You've been working hard," he observed.

Ava walked past him into the living room, to the little desk she had set up in the corner with the view of the backyard. As far as desks went, it was on the pathetic side, but it held her laptop, her small mountain of notebooks, pens, pencils and a lamp. She sat down in the chair with her back to the window, so she could keep an eye on her guest.

"I've had lots of good help," she said, gesturing to the room.

"Your friends?" he guessed, and must have been remembering the girls sorting through boxes on the floor the day he'd first showed up.

"And my mom. The guys did all the heavy lifting."

"The Dogs?"

"Yeah. My brother and all his brothers."

He nodded and folded his arms across his chest, leaning back into the sofa and rolling his head so he could look at her. This face he was making now – contemplative – didn't resemble Mercy much. It was less sharp, less reflective. It made him look more like some generic handsome man, and less like the wild creature Mercy was.

"Can I ask you a question?"

She steeled herself. "Sure."

"What do you do? I mean," he rushed to say, "are you, like, some sort of…just his wife?"

"Are you asking if I'm some sort of club commodity?" she asked drily.

"I–"

"I'm not. My father is the president. I have only ever been with one member of this club, and that's my husband." She wanted to be indignant and furious about his question, but couldn't dredge up the emotion. Frankly, she didn't care what Colin O'Donnell thought of her.

"I…" Colin swallowed, dark lashes long against his cheeks as he blinked. "Do you have a life? A real life?"

She gave him a small, thin smile. "You're supposed to be a big womanizer. What do you care?"

"Fucking a girl and never calling her back doesn't wreck her whole life."

On some level, it was touching, his show of concern. On another it was none of his business. And inwardly, she was too tired to bristle up about it. "I went to college," she said, "and I'm going to grad school."

His brows went up.

"I work when I can, but I make time for writing too. I'm a writer – that's what I do. And believe it or not, Mercy has never been anything but supportive on that front. I have a life," she said firmly. "The only one I've ever wanted."

"Hmm," he murmured, and he looked confused.

"I think," Ava went on, "that you're the one without much of a life, Colin. And I think that's why you're here."

He swallowed, and a protest darkened his face, high along his cheekbones, like Merc. "Don't take this the wrong way, darlin', but you don't know shit about me."

"You're the easiest kind of man to know," she countered. "Anonymous sex, too much beer, can't hold down a steady job – there's nothing as boring and predictable as a man who can't stand to be tied down." Quick grin. "But don't take it the wrong way," she echoed his words.

He glared at her. "Think you're real smart, don't you?"

She shrugged. "I think if you just wanted your pound of flesh, you'd have taken it and skipped town by now. You want something. And maybe you don't even know what that is, but I think you want to come to terms with the fact that you have a brother, because I think, deep down, you need him, because your mother lied to you your entire life and you don't have anyone else."

He glanced away from her, unfolding his arms and passing his hands once, twice, down the thighs of his jeans, fingers twitching.

Nerve struck.

"I also think," Ava continued, "that Mercy needs you too. You're the only blood family he has left, and even if he says that doesn't matter, I know it does. He's Southern. Hell, he's a Louisianan – family matters."

Colin's jaw clenched tight, and the silence stretched, grew thin and sharp-edged. It was quiet so long that when he spoke, it started her a little.

"You were with him?" he asked, voice strained.

"When?" she asked, but she already knew.

"When he murdered my father."

Ava took a deep breath. "I was standing right behind him." How quickly her mind went back to that terrible moment, to the cottage in Saints Hollow. How helpless she remembered being, the memory of panic leaving her legs weak and trembling. "I saw Larry through the door, standing on the porch, and there was this huge man behind him, putting a gun to his head." She pressed the tip of her forefinger to her temple though Colin wasn't looking at her. "He said he was sorry, he was so sorry, but what could he do? Mercy would have made the same decision in his place, he said. He was going to die that afternoon no matter," she said, knowing it was true, "better it be Mercy defending me than some thug punishing him."

Colin's hands curled into fists.

"He was wrong about one thing, though," she added, quietly, and Colin's head snatched around. "Mercy would never have made that decision. He would never have gone along with that plan. He would have killed them all."

A humorless snort flared Colin's sharp, Lécuyer nostrils. "He could have tried."

"No. He *would have*. That's the thing you don't know about your brother." A little shiver stole across her skin. Not fear, not revulsion, but something very much like excitement. "He's capable of *anything*. The deepest love, and the darkest violence. He doesn't try things. He does them."

He gave her a long, level stare. "You're a spooky chick, you know that?"

She twitched a grin. "It's been said a time or two."

He released a long, tired-sounding breath and let his head fall back against the couch. "I hate him for it. What he did to Dad," he said to the ceiling.

"And you don't want to hear the other side of the story," she guessed.

Other sides had a painful way of stirring up empathy.

"But…I knew there had to be one," he said, like it was an admission. "I knew…the Felix I knew growing up, anyway, wouldn't have done that without a good damn reason." His eyes flicked over to her. "Are you a good damn reason?"

"I am to him."

He looked away again. "I know."

A softening took place inside her, an urge to comfort him. He wasn't the broken glass fragments of a man that Mercy had always been, but he was hurting too. And not just because of Larry.

"You know," she said, "I have it on good authority that Mercy makes a guy a good friend."

"Like I want to be 'friends'?"

"You want to be brothers, but you're both too pig-headed to face up to the fact that Remy Lécuyer and Evie O'Donnell fooled around."

"Why the hell would I want that?"

"Because you can't forgive a friend for what happened – but you could forgive family."

He fell silent again, straightening his hands slowly and with effort as his eyes traced the stamped patterns on the ceiling.

"Did you two look alike when you were little boys?" Ava asked, careful to keep her tone low and soothing. She realized what she was doing, suddenly – she was using the same verbal approach she used with Mercy, because she was taking for granted they shared some of the same ways of thinking.

"I dunno." Colin swallowed and his Adam's apple jumped in his throat, more pronounced with his head back against the top of the cushion. "If we did, we didn't notice, I don't guess."

She wondered if Remy had looked at the boy and itched to treat him like a son also. Surely Larry had noticed that the child he raised looked more like his friend than himself. People had to have noticed; and they'd kept it from the boys all along. It struck her as cruel. All their lives with a brother, and never knowing it.

"Can I give you some advice?"

"I think you've given enough."

"Listen to what Mercy has to say," she said, undeterred. "Sit down, have a drink, and really listen to him. If you can't forgive him, then you ought to leave town. But revenge isn't going to get you anywhere."

The sound of a bike engine coming down the street was a welcome one. Ava didn't know how to bring this strange conversation to a close, and she was ready to. Get along, don't get along – she was just tired of the Colin drama. His side of it, anyway. That was the other thing about *other sides* – she didn't give a damn about anybody's side but Mercy's.

She got to her feet as the bike rolled up into the driveway and then shut off. She could tell it was Aidan, and went through the mud room to let him in.

He yanked his sunglasses off when she answered the door, already pushing past her, his hair wild and damp from being under his helmet.

"What are you–" she tried to protest as she followed his charge toward the living room. "Aidan."

He was tugging his gloves off as he found Colin sitting on the sofa, and he gestured at the guy with one, empty leather fingers slapping around in a way that made Ava want to laugh.

"Not cool, bro," Aidan told him, inhaling sharply. He was panting like he'd run a race. "Not cool." Then he pitched forward at the waist, hands on his knees, deep-breathing in earnest. "Shit," he muttered.

As Ava stepped into the room behind him, she could smell the tang of male sweat coming off her brother. "What's going on?"

"This jackass" – Aidan jabbed a finger Colin's direction as he straightened and regained a scrap of composure – "came looking for Mercy at the shop, and when I told him Merc was out picking up parts, he fucking took off." He turned a dark, Ghost-like glare on the Cajun. "What the fuck are you doing in here with my sister?"

Colin lifted both hands in a defenseless pose that looked anything but given the way his brows cranked down over his eyes. "Whoa. I didn't do shit."

"Man…" Aidan advanced on him with two charging, aggressive steps.

Ava caught him by the back of the cut, giving an insubstantial tug that he did in fact heed, pulling up short. "Hey! What's going on?"

He tried to shrug her off.

"Aidan, *explain* please."

He managed to get out of her grasp, but held his ground, glaring at Colin. "I told him Merc was coming back to the shop, and that he could wait. And instead, I turn around for two seconds, and the prospect's telling me this one just fucking left in a hurry. After I fucking *told him* not to come here, and to wait at Dartmoor. What the fuck's with that?" he demanded of Colin.

"And you assumed he'd come here."

98

"Well duh! I wanna know why, though," he growled at Colin. "What, you gonna hold my sister hostage or some shit?"

Indignation and amusement warred across Colin's face. "I just wanted to talk."

"Fucking *yeah right*, asshole."

He needs to step up his vocabulary, Ava thought. She laid a hand on her brother's arm and stepped in close to him. "We've just been talking. It's fine."

He ignored her. "You thought you'd…" He couldn't say it, whatever was making him so furious.

"Aidan." Ava slid an arm around his waist, leaned into him and felt his ribs lifting and dropping against her side. "He didn't do anything to me, I swear. Besides – I can take care of myself."

He glanced down at her, and she saw in his eyes that he was remembering the sight of the bodies in the road, the ones she'd dropped. He frowned, but he gave her a fractional nod. Yes, he knew she could look after her own safety. He remembered the New Orleans sun-drenched stretch of asphalt, and what she'd done there.

He turned back to Colin, more composed, but no less incensed. "You need to get out. If Merc isn't here–"

"He's here," Mercy's voice announced behind them, and they both spun to face him, shoulders banging together in their surprise.

Mercy stood backlit by the waning afternoon sun, and as tall as Colin was, Mercy looked mammoth in height. His leanness made him look mean, rather than less capable. As he stepped toward them, and the light fell away, his face became visible – the fury lodged the breath in Ava's throat.

"Baby," she said, reaching for him. "Everything's fine."

His eyes slid over, but he didn't move toward her. Then he looked at Aidan. "You two go to the kitchen."

Ava felt her brother's hand go around her wrist, the rough callused skin of his fingers covering her pulse. At another time, she would have marveled at the way he took orders from Mercy. But now, she was worried about blood spilling on her couch.

"Mercy." She kept her tone easy. "Colin was just waiting for you to get home. He's been behaving himself."

He didn't look at her, gaze trained on his half-brother. "Go with Aidan."

"Oh, shit," she muttered as her brother led her out of the room. "*Shit.*" She leaned a hip against the counter, standing so she had a view of what went on in the next room.

99

"What?" Aidan asked as he opened the fridge and rummaged. All the urgency had abandoned him. Now that Mercy was home, and he wasn't in charge, he didn't care what happened.

"If they get into it, Merc will kill him."

In the living room, Colin was still sitting, head tilted back at a defiant angle, and Mercy had closed the gap between them, was looming over the other man with his shoulders set at an angle Ava recognized all too well.

"So?"

"So…I probably shouldn't condone that."

Aidan snorted. "Hey, have you guys got ice cream?"

Tango had been strung-out with nerves when Mercy returned to the shop. "Now, don't freak out," had been his opening line, and then he'd told him about Colin coming – and then leaving. And that Aidan was on the way to the house to make sure Ava was alright. Tango had still been talking when Mercy turned away, strode to his bike.

Calm certainty descended. He was going to kill the man. If one hair was out of place on his Ava's head, Colin was a dead man, plain and simple.

Seeing Ava unharmed didn't do much to soothe him.

Seeing Aidan was some help. At least the guy was ready to ride to his sister's defense.

But Colin…sitting there, *again*, on his goddamn couch like he belonged there…he was done with this shit.

"Get up." It was a snarl, his voice. Nothing human about it.

Colin's dark eyes flashed, and he slowly pulled his feet down off the coffee table, one and then the other, sitting forward like he had all the time in the world. But when he spoke, he was fighting for patience. Maybe even politeness. "I just came here to talk. To you…and to her." He gestured toward the kitchen. "Thought maybe she could talk some sense into you – since she's the 'only good part of you' or whatever the hell."

"You thought" – his jaw was clenched so tight it was difficult to get the words out – "you'd get her to turn on me?"

"Whatever works."

Among his brothers, Mercy was the one lauded for his patience and restraint. Ironically. He, Walsh, and Michael had an oligarchy going when it came to thinking things through. Because torture, Mercy always argued, was a very well-thought-out endeavor, not to be rushed.

Hotheaded fistfights – he'd leave those to Aidan and the prospects, and Dublin if he'd had a few too many.

But in this moment, he was not the trusted MC extractor. He wasn't Mercy; wasn't the thoughtful brother.

He was Felix, the kid Colin had tried to leave behind during those boyhood adventures through the tangled cypress roots in their swamp playground. And Felix wanted to punch this fucker in the face.

So that's what he did.

His fist drew back and it snapped faster than Colin had expected. Faster than he'd expected himself. One second Colin was opening his mouth to say something else, and the next he was toppling off the couch onto the floor. Mercy was eighty percent sure his right hand would never be the same again after the impact with the asshole's jaw bone.

"*Fuuuuuck*," Colin hissed into the carpet as he struggled to get his hands braced beneath him. He was too unsteady, and only managed to flop around a little.

"Oh damn," Ava said from the kitchen.

"Hey!" Aidan called.

But hitting Colin had felt *good*. It had felt almost cosmic. Destined. Fated. Like forces beyond his ken had brought him together with this brother wannabe so he could complete the cycle. First father, and now son, completely at his – how perfect – *mercy*.

"Bro," Aidan said, and there were footfalls coming toward them.

"Wait," Ava said, her voice smooth, totally unruffled. His little murderer, bless her precious heart. "Maybe he needs this."

"What?" Aidan asked.

Mercy wasn't listening closely. He reached down and took a firm hold on the back of Colin's shirt, dragging up and away from the couch, out into the center of the room where he had more room to work. The guy was heavy, and Mercy saw the leap of the muscles in his arm, grunted through his teeth as he put his weight behind the pulling.

"He's going to kill him," Aidan said.

Ava was silent.

"Get the fuck off of me," Colin growled, trying to wrench free. He dug his fingers into the rug and kicked at Mercy's shin. Moving him was like hauling a mature bull gator up into a boat. Remy had always been so good at that – getting the flopping dead gators into the boat. All by himself, without benefit of a wench, he could drag those big ones up over the side, sweat pouring down his dark, smiling face, scarred arms bulging with the effort.

Good ol' Daddy. The best daddy there ever could have been. Doting on little Felix and taking good care of his mama.

And fucking Evie O'Donnell.

Making a second son he kept secret.

A terrible sound swelled in the room as Mercy fell on the man his father had sired in secret. Colin was scrambling onto his back and swinging fists and presenting a picture of a big man ready to inflict violence. His face twisted up in a snarl and he came up off the carpet at Mercy with the kind of menace that sent men to their knees.

For Mercy it was nothing. He wasn't seeing Colin, the room, the logic behind any of it. All he could see was his father's dazzling white smile as he sat back in the boat and said, "Whew! Lord, that was a big one. Good shootin', Felix. That's my boy!"

A lie – such a big lie – and how many other lies had he missed? How much had Remy hidden from him?

His father! He'd named his son for him. He'd buried the man with his own two hands in the shade of the oak trees beyond the house.

And this living, breathing lie, accusing him of murder, coming into his house, talking to his wife.

Mercy hit him again, and again, straddling him when he fell, driving his fist into his all-too-familiar face over and over.

Blood on the carpet.

Blood on his knuckles.

Those dark Remy eyes swollen and bloodied, so they didn't look so much like Remy anymore.

At some point, Mercy realized the noise in the room was his own incoherent screaming. An awful wordless growling that he couldn't seem to hold inside his chest.

How do you like that, Colin? I turned out bigger than you. I turned out better than you. Daddy loved me, and he died at the hands of a man I cut the tattoos off of to prove how much I loved him back.

He couldn't breathe. The scream was strangling him. And Colin wasn't moving much anymore.

Then there was a hand. A single, cool hand against the back of his neck, curled lightly, echoing the shape of his throat. He would know those skinny white fingers anywhere, just by feel.

He sat back suddenly, drawing in a huge breath that burned his lungs.

Ava's hand went down to his shoulder. He felt her hair brush the side of his face as she leaned toward him, kissed his temple, let her lips skim his ear.

"Baby, stop," she said quietly. "You don't want to kill him."

"I do." His own voice was raw and strained.

Colin's chest lifting beneath him was the only evidence of life.

"No," Ava murmured. She petted his hair, ran her hand along the crown of his head. "Come on. Let's clean you up. Aidan can take care of him."

He wanted to finish it. He did. He wanted to end this family that had tried to end his. The family that had sent gunmen through the swamp to get to his wife and the child she carried.

But when Ava's skinny-fingered hand slid around his bicep, he stood at her slightest urging, and he let her draw him back.

"Aidan," she said in that composed, businesslike voice she'd inherited from her mother. "Can you do something about this?"

Aidan was staring at Colin slack-jawed. "Um...yeah."

It always worked this way, didn't it? He carved them up and his brothers took care of disposal. He thought of Ronnie Archer and Mason Stephens, their limp dead bodies sagging against the duct tape, the prospects coming in with gloves and bleach and plastic bags, Walsh taking notes off to the side. He was not the disposer – he was the punisher. Pain was his trade. Torture was his value.

And so he let Ava steer him down the hall to the bathroom.

She was probably a bad hostess, and Aidan was probably making a mess of things, but Ava refused to be a part of whatever shuffling and grunting and cussing was going on out in the living room. She'd heard several bikes and a truck pull up, and overlapping male voices talked about what they should do before it sounded like the lot of them left, and all the engines fired up again.

Thank God Colin was out of the house finally.

Mercy sat on the side of the tub in the master bathroom, so still he didn't seem to be breathing. His knuckles were a bloody mess and she knelt before him, cleaning them gently with a damp washcloth, trying to get beneath Colin's blood to see how bad the damage was to the hand.

"Does that hurt?" she asked, dabbing the splits in the skin.

"No."

She reached back onto the counter for the alcohol. "This is going to, though. Sorry."

"S'alright."

She winced in anticipation as she flooded a clean square of the cloth with alcohol and started dabbing again.

Mercy, as expected, took it stoically, a sharp inhale through his nostrils the only sign of discomfort. He kept his hands very still in her grasp, letting her clean each abrasion thoroughly.

She smeared a thin layer of triple antibiotic ointment across the marks and stood, wiping her hands off on her jeans. "That should do it."

He curled his hands into fists and his brows crimped as the split skin pulled tight over the knuckles. "Thanks, baby."

"You hungry?" she asked as she put the first aid supplies under the sink. "We've got leftover Alfredo bake if you want some. I can heat it up."

She detected the energy rolling off him in the moment of stillness before he spoke. She felt the shift in his tightly-reined anger, the way it turned to something else, tangible as the low vibration of a TV in another room.

"You're not gonna say anything?" he asked.

Ava glanced at him over her shoulder and saw coiled tension in his large body, as he leaned forward and braced his forearms on his thighs, gaze trained on her. "Why? You don't want to hear anything."

A thin smile touched one corner of his mouth. "You're not gonna guilt-trip me about putting my brother in a coma?"

Finished, she set the washcloth on the counter and leaned a hip against it. "Are we admitting that's who he is now?" she asked softly.

His face tightened, throat jumping as he swallowed.

"I don't wanna talk about it right now."

"I know."

"I want—"

"I know what you want." The same thing he always wanted after he'd been violent: her.

She didn't brace herself against him. Even though he came up off the tub like a shot and closed the gap between them like a damn Mack truck, she knew he'd be gentle with her, and he was. His hands were soft manacles around her wrists, and she fell into the dance as if they'd rehearsed the steps. Around, putting her back to the wall, hands going to his shoulders as his head ducked and his mouth crashed down onto hers.

A feral, feverish kiss. His hands at the button of her jeans, the zipper.

When he hoisted her up against the wall, she wrapped her bare legs tight around his hips and dug her nails into the rigid muscles beneath his shirt. It was deep, insistent penetration, and his breath was loud and coarse against her neck as he channeled the blood lust into this sweeping need to be inside her.

Like a child seeking comfort, she thought. That bit of shame and confusion and self-hatred over what he'd done. And the life-affirming succor he wanted afterward, needed by the broken child in him, taken by the virile man.

He cursed, and then tensed, and then stilled, the orgasm locking him up tight, a full-body spasm.

Ava pushed her hands through his hair, kissed his throat and said, "Take me to bed. Do me right."

"I will."

And then she was going to talk to him about his brother.

Ten
Dear Brother

After two days of putting it off, it was time to go see Colin.

Mercy was far from flush in the cash department, but he probably could have swung a brief stay at the Holiday Inn.

Not so with Colin, apparently. According to Aidan, the guy had directed them to the old one-story, empty-pool-in-the-parking-lot Road King Motel off the interstate. The place looked even sadder than he remembered. Thick cracks spidering across the pavement, sprouting tufted grass. Kudzu had claimed the south wall. The roofline sagged, missing shingles flashing like gapped teeth. The cars in the parking lot were all two decades old, save Colin's Jeep.

The once-brass number for room six was crusty with some sort of corrosion that looked like moss. Mercy knocked hard and waited.

Knocked again.

There was shuffling on the other side. Colin's voice was rough in the way of guys who'd had the shit beat out of them. "What?"

"It's Felix. Open up."

"I can see it's you through the damn peephole. Ugly-ass."

"Prettier than you." He pushed his hair back for show. "You gonna open the door or what?"

"Am I gonna have to defend myself?"

Mercy sighed. "Just open the door."

Sound of the security chain dropping away, deadbolt turning.

The door swung inward and the evening sunlight slanted in over Mercy's shoulders, striking Colin's battered face like a stage spotlight. The swelling was terrible. Left eye swollen shut, the right a mere glittering crescent between the puffy lids. Lots of ugly bruising that would darken to blue and green. Split lip.

Mercy was used to seeing the damage his fists left behind – but the remorse was a new sensation.

Colin stepped aside with a mock-gallant sweep of his arm, inviting him into the dim room.

"All the comforts of home," Mercy said as he took quick visual stock.

Color scheme from the seventies: mustard yellow, avocado green, shit brown. The sagging double mattress was draped with a threadbare comforter printed with yellow, green, and brown flowers.

106

Lucite side tables. Boxy console TV with a faded silk flower arrangement on top. The carpet was yellow, and shag, and stained in too many places to mention. Mercy took a deep breath and pulled the dark scent of mildew down into his lungs.

He turned as Colin shut the door. "There a reason you had to do the whole cliché dive motel thing?"

Colin shrugged and sat down on the foot of the bed. The mattress groaned. "It's cheap."

"You hurting for money?"

They hadn't moved beyond the living room beatdown, but they were both, through unspoken agreement, going to put it on the back burner for the moment.

Colin shrugged again. "I'm between jobs. I'll find something else. It's not me I'm worried about." His voice hardened, eyes lifting to Mercy.

Shit.

"Evie's having a rough time of it?"

"She's flat broke."

The news landed heavy as a bag of sand across his shoulders. "Damn." He dropped into the stiff-backed chair closest to the door. "They didn't have anything stashed away in savings?"

"Nah. Mom was all about enjoying what they could while they had it."

And now she had nothing.

Mercy massaged the sore knuckles of his right hand. Guilt made the soreness worse.

"And it's my fault she's in bad shape," he said, and Colin didn't argue.

Ava's words from two days before came back to him. After he'd taken her up against the bathroom wall, and then taken her more thoroughly, in their bed. *"If you can't make peace with him, you can at least say you wish Larry wasn't dead, because you do wish that."*

He sighed. She was right. Wasn't she always? So much for his age giving him an advantage in the wisdom department.

"I never shoulda called them."

"Why did you?"

"Because…" It was easier than he wanted it to be to go back to that headspace. The grating anxiety, the obsessive need to keep his *fillette* safe. "Because I needed friends," was the only way he knew how to say it. "And I didn't trust anyone the way I trusted Larry and Evie."

Colin stared at him.

"I asked them to check and see if Saints Hollow was occupied," he continued. "And they were the ones who offered to stock the fridge and make up the bed. They went above and beyond – as always." He swallowed hard. "And then they sold us out. And when it came down to turning myself over, letting Ava fall into enemy hands – I made the only choice I could. It was a shit choice, but so were all the others. We weren't all going to make it out of that swamp alive. I had to pick who walked away whole – and I picked my woman, and I picked myself, so I could get her home safe. Hate me for it if you want – you're entitled to it. But all I did was pick. You would have had to, if it'd been you."

Colin studied his boots, which Mercy took as a good sign.

When it stayed quiet, Mercy said, "Evie never told you, did she?"

Flicker of lashes as dark eyes searched the room.

"That Larry wasn't your old man."

A line of tension unfurled between them, humming with the strain of holding onto each of them.

And then it snapped.

Colin heaved a deep, weary sigh. "She did. Right before I drove up here."

"Yeah?"

"She told me what happened. Then, the morning I left, she got up all hysterical and crying in her bathrobe. Sat me down, told me about…" He swallowed. "Remy. She thought I'd come up here and hurt you. 'Don't kill your brother,' she told me.' " He snorted. "Didn't say anything about you killing me."

Mercy felt a faint smile tug at his mouth. "Yeah, well, Evie doesn't know what I do for a living."

Colin's brows went up. "Fix bikes?" he asked, mockingly.

"Far as you know." Suddenly, he was exhausted. He slumped down in his chair, legs spread to hold his weight. "Look – I never liked you growing up. You were a shit."

Colin twitched a grin.

"Still are. I thought little brothers were supposed to be respectful. Reverent, even."

"You're shit outta luck there."

"Obviously. But no matter what I thought about you, you've gotta believe that I always loved Larry and Evie. I hate what happened. Shit, I *hate* it. But…I wouldn't change what I did in that moment. This life…" The way he was slouched, he could read the patches down the front of his cut. "It doesn't lend itself to happy endings."

Colin was quiet for a long moment, picking at loose threads on the knee of his jeans, the fading sunlight painting his battered face in gruesome bas relief. "It's not like it is in movies, is it?"

"No."

His head lifted, and even though he only had part of one eye open, Mercy could read the intensity of his gaze. "The guys who killed Remy...you took care of them?"

"Big Son bait."

Colin nodded. Glanced toward the window. "You know," he mused. "You were always a scrawny, weird kid. I didn't think you'd turn out bigger than me."

"You tend to miss stuff when you're stuck so far up your own ass."

"Yeah."

"Both our fathers are dead. I don't see much of a reason to keep on putting people in the ground on their behalf."

Colin took a deep, deep breath...and let it out in a rush. "Yeah."

The shadows stretched. Evening birdsong filtered through the window, light and trilling. Evidence that the world turned and retained its beauty, despite the ugliness of men.

"You know," Colin said, easing back so he rested on his elbows, his frame relaxed now, the last aggression bleeding out of him. "I have no idea what it's like to care about shit the way you do."

Mercy smiled. "Hurts like hell, but it's worth it."

He thought of what awaited him at home: the magic of his girl and their boy that kept him from self-destructing on a daily basis.

"You got enough money to get wherever you wanna go next?"

Shame-faced, Colin shook his head.

"I think I can help with that." Then, on impulse: "What are you eating for dinner?"

"Whatever they got in the vending machine."

"Come back to the house with me. We've got leftovers, but they're warm, and homemade."

"Oh...okay."

Eleven
Girls Gone Wild

"I have grapes. Do you want some?" Holly asked as she popped the plastic lid off the Glad container of fruit she'd packed. There was a full-size fridge in the Dartmoor trucking office, and she was making a point of packing nutritious lunches. Usually, what had sounded good at six that morning while she was prepping no longer sounded good by lunchtime, but she made herself eat anyway. Lots of vitamins, protein, and calcium.

Most days, much to her delight, Michael wandered over from the body shop and ate with her. So she always packed enough for both of them, sure to include things he liked – iced down red Gatorade on a hot day, chocolate-dipped granola bars, peppered tomato sandwiches.

That's what he was eating today: sliced red tomatoes on wheat, light mayo, lettuce, red onion, and lots of pepper. Holly thought they were disgusting; Michael's eyes always brightened in silent thanks when she presented him with one.

He regarded the red grapes from his chair across the desk and then reached for a bunch, transferring them to his paper plate.

Things had been warm, and simple, and easy between them since the rope incident, their particular brand of intimacy revived not by the sex, but the truths traded afterward. Holly felt a small measure of triumph – they'd had a marital awkward moment, and they'd pushed past it. It was so normal and boring and…wonderful.

"What's that?" he asked, nodding toward the tidy stack of handwritten pages she'd left beside the keyboard.

She was distracted a moment by his tongue curling around a grape and plucking it off the stem, then refocused. "It's one of Ava's stories. One of her old ones. Sam found a box of them while we were unpacking, and she said we could read them, if we wanted." She gestured to the tomblike office around them. "We were having a quiet day, so…" She shrugged.

"Can she write worth a damn?"

Holly frowned. "I don't have much to compare her to, really. But…" She pressed her lips together as she stared at the handwritten cover of the story. She'd worried, at first, that she'd be unable to identify with the characters in any story. Not that she wouldn't like them or understand them, but that she would have no idea what they were talking about.

But on page one, she'd been sucked in. The office had faded around her as she tumbled into the life of a girl trying to find her place in a cruel, unsympathetic world. The phone had rung three times before she noticed it.

"I think she's good," she said, glancing back at Michael. "You could probably read it, if you wanted to."

He shook his head emphatically and picked up his sandwich. "Nope. Not reading something somebody else's old lady wrote."

She laughed. "Why not?"

He sighed, elbows braced on the desk, sandwich dripping pink tomato juice onto the plate. "Because if she's writing about…what she wants to do to Mercy or something" – he shifted in his seat – "and I read it, that's…a violation, or something." He frowned at his own awkwardness and Holly bit back her smile. "No."

"Okay, fair enough."

A silhouette swept past the closed blinds before the door was pushed open. Holly was sad to have their lunch interrupted, but she hitched herself upright in her chair when she spotted Maggie.

Michael saw her stiffen and turned to look over his shoulder, dismissing the head old lady with a fast nod and going back to his food.

Maggie was in a loose A-line peach-colored sleeveless top and denim Bermuda shorts, leather flip-flops, blonde hair wavy and thick over her shoulders. She looked like she'd just walked off a beach somewhere.

"Hey, you busy in here?"

Holly shook her head. "It's been quiet."

"Can you take the rest of lunch and come help me? Jasmine's supposed to be taking inventory at the clubhouse, and I need to go verify before I send her shopping."

Holly nodded and pushed her chair back. She didn't want anything to do with the Lean Bitches, but when the groupies were put in charge of housekeeping, it necessitated contact sometimes. And she wasn't about to tell Maggie no. "Sure."

Sorry, she mouthed to Michael as Maggie turned her back on them.

He shrugged…but his eyes said he'd miss her company.

She dropped an impulsive kiss on his forehead on her way out.

On a good day, when asked, Jasmine would say that she much preferred her status as most important Lean Bitch to that of a club old lady. She would have said that she was her own mistress, with no one ragging on her about dinner and cold beer in the fridge, with a bed all to herself when she chose, and plenty of company when she didn't. The old ladies were the wives; she was the exciting, exotic thrill. The old ladies waited hand and foot on just one man; she had Tango, and Aidan, and Candy when he was in town – not to mention those three little new prospects weren't so little where it counted. She would have said that she was a sexual creature, and she could never tolerate being someone's little missus.

These were all flagrant lies, of course, but who had to know that save her and the pillow that accepted her tears at the end of the day? She had, after all, chosen this road. She'd ride it – literally, most of the time – without too much bitching. Her poor grandmother was spinning in her grave somewhere; her mother was…wherever she'd gone off to twenty years ago. And she was in charge of kitchen inventory at the clubhouse, because despite the suck-fest that was her personal life, she did love all her boys, and she liked cooking for them.

"Seriously?" she asked herself, surveying the clubhouse pantry with hands on hips. Nothing but Oreos, potato chips, and boxes of taco shells stared back at her from the shelves. "Bottom of the barrel."

There was a notepad and pen on the counter, and she began a list that was basically from scratch, given the current state of supplies. They needed bread, pasta, rice, ground beef, luncheon meat, olives, hot dogs…

A light rap on the doorjamb pulled her attention, and she glanced up. "Yeah?"

The woman standing in the threshold wasn't anyone she'd expected to see again. The shy brunette who'd responded to the online dating profile she'd set up for Tango. Today, she was wearing painted-on jeans and a purple tank top; her hair was shiny and flat-ironed, dark sheets down her back. Heavy makeup, lots of perfume. She propped one foot up on its toes and cocked her hip in a pose that managed to be both hesitant and bold.

"Hi," she said, a slow mile curving her lips.

"Hi," Jasmine echoed, without emotion.

"The, uh, the guy out front said you were back here."

That would be Littlejohn, mopping the floor. Jasmine felt an instant stab of irritation that he'd given some random chick directions back here to the kitchen. Yeah, they'd had a fun afternoon, but she was busy. And she didn't want to make a habit of helping doe-eyed things discover their kinky sides.

"Yeah, well" – the smile was fake and surely the other girl could tell that – "I've got kind of a busy day, so…" She made a dismissive gesture, flicking her fingers toward the door.

Little Doe didn't get it. "Is Tango here?" She took a step inside the kitchen, hand braced on the jamb, attempting that pose that turned a woman's body into an enticing sequence of curves.

"No." Jasmine turned back to her list. Canned corn, canned peas, canned baked beans. "I've got no idea where he is." She hadn't seen him at all that day, come to think of it; she'd glimpsed him swinging a leg over his bike about eleven, but to her knowledge, he wasn't back yet. That was a *long* lunch.

Soft scuffing footsteps told her the girl came into the room and moved to stand beside her. She could hear her breathing through her mouth, quick, excited little breaths. "Is he coming back? Will he be here in a little while?"

"Dunno." Jasmine lifted her head and was startled by how close the brunette was, hovering right at her elbow.

The girl smiled nervously, chewing at her lip. "Maybe…maybe we could wait for him. You and me." Uncertain laugh. "We could…get started. And then he could join us."

"What? Like, you and me?"

More lip chewing, emphatic nodding, a certain hazy glazed desire clouding the girl's eyes.

"Oh, honey," Jasmine sighed, "that's real flattering, but the other day, that was just a one-time thing."

She was totally crestfallen, brows plucking together, teeth catching hard in her lip. "But Tango…"

"Sweetie" – she wasn't trying to be patronizing, it was just happening – "Tango isn't big on change. What we did before – that's not gonna be a regular thing." Nor did she want it to be, she realized. It was shocking to feel the way jealousy tightened her gut. For the most part, she knew that Tango – fragile, gentle baby boy that he was – needed an old lady. He needed a wife, who was devoted, who understood his unspoken hang-ups. But there was a part of her that wasn't ready to let him go, and that part of her was pissed the hell off that this chick had showed up.

"But, the ad said—"

"Yeah, I know, but I wrote the ad. Tango had nothing to do with it. I thought – well, I thought wrong, okay? And he's not here."

"But—"

"Look, I can tell him you came by, and if he's interested, I can call you. Maybe we could..." *Not gonna happen*, she thought, but there was so sense crushing her.

There was a quick, dark glimmer in the girl's eyes, something other than the hope and reticence she'd shown so far. "Call him," she suggested, voice hardening a fraction. "Call and see if he's coming back soon."

Jasmine shook her head. "Sorry, honey, I'm not his keeper." She bent her head over the grocery list again – and a tinny warning sound pulsed in the back of her mind. A metallic *ping, ping, ping*, like sonar bleeping in sea monster movies.

"Um..." the girl said. "What?"

"I'm not calling him. I'm not bothering him with this."

"Bothering him?" The girl's voice twisted, became shrill. "I responded to the ad. *I* came *here*. Because he wanted me. How is that fucking bothering?"

Some self-possessed women cursed with a natural fluency, that sounded neither vulgar nor out of place. Women like Maggie Teague. But *fuck* coming out of this girl's mouth sounded raw and nasty. It startled Jasmine, brought her head up with a jerk. "What?"

The girl's eyes were bright with unshed tears. Her lips quivered over clenched teeth and her cheeks colored with anger. "I'm bothering *you*, right? Not him. He doesn't even know I'm here, and you won't tell him, because I'm bothering *you*."

Jasmine lifted a placating hand. "Don't get all upset, okay? This isn't personal–"

"Yes it is!" the girl snapped. "After what I...what we..." Her cheeks flushed darkly and she batted her lashes. "It *was* personal."

Oh, this was so not supposed to have happened. Right about the time that girl's hand had slipped under Jasmine's skirt, she should have realized this wasn't a one true love situation.

"No," Jasmine said, as gently as she could. "That was just fun. That was just crazy sex."

The brunette *snarled*. Actually snarled, like an angry dog, and Jasmine staggered back a step, the alarms screaming in her head now. "Are you rejecting me?"

"I'm saying there's nothing here for you. Go home."

"Call Tango!" the girl shouted, and it was an awful sound. "I want to talk to him, not you."

Jasmine took another step back and felt the pantry door bump into her shoulder. "You need to calm down, and think about what you're saying," she said in as soothing a voice as she could manage, given the anxious flutter in her chest. "You came here and got naked with two strangers. How did you think that was going to play out? Did you think we'd, like, date you or something?"

Wrong thing to say.

"If it were up to me, I'd just give her a credit card and send her, but Ghost wants me to go over the list and pre-load the club debit account with the cash, let her use that," Maggie explained as they walked across the shimmering mirages on the Dartmoor asphalt. "The woman's been the designated shopper for years, but oh no, boss man can't trust anybody."

"Well…" Holly didn't have an answer to that. Personally, she wasn't very trusting of the groupie who'd mistaken her for one of her own the night they'd met. To be fair, she didn't know her. And to be more fair, it wasn't her business – if Maggie had faith in the woman, then she ought to as well. The Lean Dogs MC was a massive organization, and if Jasmine was a cog in the mechanics, then Holly could be thankful for her help.

"One of the other girls," Maggie continued, not noticing Holly's noncommittal answer, "is supposed to be doing a housekeeping inventory. Bleach, Lysol, that kinda stuff. Here." She handed a printed-out list to Holly. "If you can add this to what she's got, that'd be great."

Holly took it. "Sure thing."

The interior of the clubhouse was a cool, dark respite from the heat outside, their footsteps echoing hollowly off the hardwood floor in the common room. It smelled fresh – lemon cleanser, wood polish – and Holly took a deep breath of the AC-chilled air.

"Jasmine?" Maggie called, surveying the quiet room. Packed wall-to-wall during multi-chapter parties, it seemed cavernous now. "You in here?"

No answer.

"Come on." Maggie fanned herself with the list she carried, honeyed hair rustling. "She must be back here."

Holly followed her down the hall toward the kitchen –

And they both froze.

"Hey!" someone shouted.

A gasp.

A grunt.

A half-strangled scream.

Scuffling.

Maggie's hand fluttered back, grabbed at Holly's wrist. *Hold tight*, her squeeze said. *Stay right here with me.* It struck Holly as maternal, and she tucked in close behind the matriarch as they peered around the edge of the doorjamb into the kitchen.

Holly bit down hard on a gasp.

There was a brunette woman she'd never seen before with her hands wrapped around Jasmine's throat. Jasmine was no fainting flower, and she clawed at the woman's hands, kicked and bowed against the pressure at her throat. But clearly, the other woman had gotten the drop on her, and her face was a terrifying shade of purple as she struggled for air.

Maggie sucked in a deep breath.

Holly watched the brunette's thumbs dig into Jasmine's windpipe.

"Hey!" Maggie shouted, stepping forward.

The brunette let go of Jasmine with one hand and reached lightning-fast into her purse, coming back out with a small, gleaming knife that she brandished toward the Lean Dogs queen.

"Jesus, are you insane?" Maggie demanded. "Jazz, what the hell is going on?"

Jasmine's eyes were huge, tear-brightened, and she said nothing, lips trembling.

"This isn't your business," the brunette hissed, gesturing with the knife.

"Oh, you've got to be kidding me," Maggie said, stepping back, hands help up to show that they were empty. "Jasmine, what the hell is going on?"

Jasmine pulled in a deep breath, but only air left her lips afterward. She was either too petrified to speak, or worried whatever she said would launch the brunette's knife toward her.

"Get back," the brunette told Maggie. She shifted sideways, so she had Jasmine up against the fridge with her right hand, the left extending the knife toward the old lady.

She didn't seem to see Holly.

Which meant Holly had a choice to make, and a split second to act. She might not have been part of Jasmine's cheering section, but the woman was loyal to the club, and was valued for it. And then Maggie – well, she was the queen bee, the president's wife, the mother of the first friend Holly had ever had in her life.

And she was no stranger to violence. She was well-acquainted with it, actually.

116

Holly slipped around the corner, into the storage room, and took one of the collapsed folding chairs in both hands. She didn't hesitate on her way back – she might lose her nerve if she did. She swung around the doorjamb, brought the chair up –

And cracked the strange brunette across the back of the head with the aluminum chair as hard as she could.

The sound echoed inside the small kitchen. Like a gong ringing.

The girl's head flew back, neck going limp, eyes rolling toward the ceiling. She collapsed to the floor in a boneless heap.

Holly glanced up, chair still held up high against her chest.

Jasmine and Maggie stared at her, eyes huge, totally speechless.

Holly dampened her lips. "Was I not supposed to do that?"

Tango didn't see the text until he arrived at the bike shop. Burning with guilt already, he hopped off his bike, raked his fingers through his hair, pulled his phone out of his pocket....and stopped breathing.

It was from Maggie: *Something's happened w/ Jasmine. She won't say, but I think she wants you.*

"Christ," he whispered, lifting his head, scanning the open roll-top doors in front of him. He'd taken a two-hour lunch. He couldn't afford to dally anymore. But his heart was thundering as he tried to work out what "something's happened" meant.

Aidan and Carter were crouched in front of a shiny blue Bob loaded with saddlebags and flying a raccoon tail and an American flag off the back. Sponsor and prospect had their heads close together as Aidan pointed something out in the engine with a grimy finger and Carter nodded his understanding. The kid was turning out to be a good little mechanic. And he was a strong prospect: polite, responsive, respectful, but he had a personality under his pretty-boy looks and he let it shine through when he thought he could.

They were busy, distracted; they'd done without him this long, what was five more minutes to check on Jazz?

He took off toward the clubhouse at a jog. And then broke into a run.

God. Had she...? Was she...? A dozen possibilities spun through his mind, each more horrible than the last.

He saw a cluster of people standing under the pavilion, and headed that way, out of breath by the time he drew up behind Maggie.

She turned to face him. "That was quick."

He gave her a cursory glance, eyes skipping wild. "Where is she? What happened?"

Maggie stepped back with a small, smirking sort of smile. "I'll let her explain it."

Sitting on the bench, between Holly and Harry the prospect, Jasmine had a damp cloth pressed to her throat and cupped her forehead with the other hand, looking frightened and exhausted. Her eyes came up to him and there was fear glimmering in their depths. The foreignness of it – he'd never seen her scared – nearly took his legs out from under him.

Harry jumped up, hands fidgeting nervously at his sides, the smattering of freckles across his nose bright against his pale, nervous face. "I'm gonna go check and see if Littlejohn got her to the hospital alright."

"That's a good idea," Maggie told him before he jogged off.

Holly stood like she was nervous, brows crimped as she took one last look at Jasmine and then excused herself.

Maggie touched his shoulder. "I'll be at the office if you need anything. The prospects took care of the girl."

What girl? he wanted to ask, but his tongue was glued to the roof of his mouth as he stared at Jasmine, the vivacious groupie slumped over like a wilted flower.

Groupie. He hated that word. It implied an ugliness of spirit that he refused to ascribe to this woman who, in so many ways, had eased him into this MC world.

"Jazz." He sat down heavily beside her because his knees wouldn't support him any longer, and he laid a hand in the middle of her back, rubbing lightly at the sensitive place just above her bra clasp. "Darling," he said, because he'd heard that word so many times; never *darlin'*, but the unabridged, crisp, proper version. "What happened?"

She sighed and pulled the cloth away, holding it in her lap. He saw the angry red marks around her neck and he wanted to scream.

Who had done this? One of his brothers? Someone wanting to take things too far?

But Maggie had said "girl."

"Jazz."

She let out a long, shaky breath, and turned a halfhearted smile toward him. "You know how you didn't want to try the online dating thing? Turns out you were right."

He stared at her stupidly.

"Our little guest of honor from the other day? Yeaaahhhh…turns out she's a clingy psycho. She showed up looking for us." She grimaced, teeth catching at her lower lip. "And when I told her it wasn't gonna happen again she kinda…strangled me."

"What the *hell?*" The words exploded out of him.

"Yeah, she, um, she had a knife too. She pulled it on Mama Mags and I–" She shook her head, shuddering hard. "I think she would have killed one of us, T, I really do." She lifted her eyes to his, her lashes clumpy with unshed tears. "God, I had no idea something like this could – I just – I'm so sorry. So, so sorry."

Tango eased his arm around her and pulled her into his side, hugging her close. His heart stuttered and his breath stalled out, but he managed a calm voice. "It's okay. You didn't know." He tried to inhale and his chest ached. "The important thing is no one got hurt. You're okay, right?"

She nodded against his shoulder. "Yeah, I'm fine." Then, to his surprise, she let out a weak chuckle. "You shoulda seen Michael's little mouse Holly. She hit that bitch in the back of the head with a chair. Knocked her right out."

Tango leaned back. "She *what?*"

Smiling now, Jasmine disentangled herself from him and lifted both hands as if she held something, miming the action. "Bong! I mean, I had no idea that girl could swing like that."

"Holly?"

"Oh yeah. And then she was just all, 'Oh no,' or something like that. But it didn't even *phase* her." She laughed again, stronger this time. "I give her props – I had no idea there was a badass under all that sugar."

Tango had a hard time visualizing it, but then again, the woman had married Michael. She couldn't be that naïve. "What happened to the girl?"

"The prospect was taking her to the ER. In the next county over. Gonna tell them he found her in the street."

He nodded, wishing they'd had her arrested, knowing no one at the station would have believed Jasmine's side of things.

"Are you sure you're okay?" He reached to smooth her hair back. "God, it scared the hell out of me when I saw Mags' text. I just…" Didn't want to put that kind of fear and guilt into words.

"Tango Estes" – her voice was bright, her eyes terribly sad – "do you love me or something?"

"I do."

"Oh, baby boy," she sighed, leaning into his shoulder, looping her arm through his. "That's not love. Not the real kind."

He snorted. "There's a real kind?"

"Yeah."

"And what's that look like?"

"I'm not real sure, 'cause I ain't ever been a part of it, you know. But I guess it looks something like the boss and Mama Mags. Mercy and that little baby wife of his. I dunno."

"Hmph."

It was quiet a beat. "I want that for you," she said, softly. "I want you to be happy."

"I do love you," he protested, but it sounded hollow.

"I know you do, baby, but love doesn't always make you happy." She tilted her head back, so she could see his face. "I know you love me, but you don't *love* me. I want you to *love*; I want it to fill you up and make you warm." She gave him a sincere, sideways smile. "And real doesn't mean anything or anyone in particular – it just means *real*. Whatever's most real for you."

Her eyes held his tight and he felt their pale depths were sending him some silent communication. Like she could see inside his head; like she'd properly interpreted all that early trauma he'd been carrying with him those first few nights she pulled him down between the sheets to lie with her in a cramped dorm bed.

Jasmine was no dummy. She knew, he realized with a lurching grab in his stomach. She knew, or she suspected the things that had happened to him before Ghost had hung a cut from his shoulders.

He shifted, glancing away from her, skin feeling too tight suddenly.

"Jazz–"

"You smell nice," she whispered. "Like something real fancy, the kinda stuff they keep in pretty bottles under glass cases."

He swallowed a rising knot of panic. "Jazz–"

She kissed the side of his throat, lips against his frantic pulse. "Baby, hush, I'd never tell a soul. Did you think I didn't guess it? You all nervous as a teenage girl." There was nothing of insult in her voice.

He screwed his eyes shut tight, until it hurt with the effort. "I'm not–" he said through his teeth. "I'm a Lean Dog, and I'm *not*–"

"Oh, sweet boy." She petted his hair, fingertips light against his scalp. "I know how the club works. I would never tell. I don't care who you've been, or what you are."

"But I'm *not*."

"I know, I know." Her voice grew thready and cracked; he could hear the tears in it. "Baby boy, I know."

**

It was the next day that Tango came to thank Holly. When he appeared in the propped-open doorway of the trucking office, hands shoved in his pockets, the sun haloing around him, Holly saw how very pretty he was, under the tattoos, the funky hair, and all the piercings. Pretty like the male runway models she'd seen in magazines. Fine-boned, and boyish, and innocent-looking, in one of those unguarded moments in which a person revealed the under-layers of himself without meaning to.

"Hi," she said, smiling, and waved him in. "I'm just organizing receipts for the cabinet. You can come in."

Whether it was the prettiness, or the touch of nerves between his crimped brows, something about him was completely disarming, and he didn't stir up her usual anxieties about being alone with men.

He glanced down at the scuffed toes of his boots as he entered, giving her ample time to study him. His garage shirt hung off his thin shoulders. He had lean hands with long fingers; the backs of them, between the first and second knuckle, were tattooed with realistic-looking domino tiles; the black dots on them seemed to be actual depressions, the shading was done so well. Both arms were intricately tattooed, and on the inside of his left forearm, she saw a flower. A delicate white bloom. A jasmine flower.

When he was in front of the desk, his head lifted, and his gaze was direct, soft, and full of emotion. "I wanted to come thank you, for saving Jazz the yesterday."

"I wouldn't say *save*."

"I would. I've seen some really awful, crazy shi – stuff happen, and lots of times, there's no one around brave enough to do anything about it. She could have–" He cleared his throat. "So thank you. She's real important to me and I…thank you."

Holly smiled, tenderness unfurling in her chest. She wanted to protest, to wave off his earnest insistence. But she said, "You're very welcome."

As he left, Maggie entered, and Holly figured the woman had been waiting around the corner, listening to Tango's expression of gratitude.

"Afternoon," the blonde greeted as she came to take the chair across from the desk, legs crossed at a casual angle.

"Good afternoon," Holly echoed, tensing in anticipation of whatever this would bring about. She knew she was being tested by the biker queen, and she didn't resent the woman for it. When Michael asked if the other old ladies were kind to her, she always said they were, because this was a tricky female thing and she didn't want him

121

blundering his awkward way into it. He would have interfered out of love, but it would have still been an interference.

"So…." Maggie said, examining her fingernails. They were painted a bright summer white. "The boys have a run coming up."

"To New Hampshire in two weeks." Her throat ached at the thought. They would leave a skeleton crew behind, but Michael, as sergeant at arms, would go along to protect his president.

Maggie nodded. "Right. Well, usually, when they're gone for a few days, we girls get together and have a potluck." Her eyes flipped up to Holly, stern and serious. "You ought to come."

Holly went very still. "Really?"

Maggie gave her a fractional smile. "Hey, sometimes you gotta conk a bitch over the head with something. I get that. You should come, yeah."

Twelve
Take My Blood

The best day of the week was, by far, Sunday. The baby still woke early, wanting to be fed, but there was no rush otherwise. When his fussy cries filtered through the baby monitor, Mercy climbed from bed and brought him back. Ava nursed him as dawn broke over the house and they lay drowsily on the pillows, talking about small, unimportant little things like saving for a new sofa and what they wanted for dinner.

Today had been exquisite in its ordinary, uneventful complacency. Often, they'd head to her parents' for dinner, but earlier that afternoon, Mercy had rubbed a slab of pork with spices and dropped it in the slow cooker with vinegar and a little broth. By the time the evening shadows stretched long and thin across the floorboards, the whole house was redolent with smoky paprika and garlic.

Ava was strapping Remy into his baby swing when Mercy said, "He needs a brother."

The buckle clicked into place and she turned, still crouched on the floor, glancing with disbelief toward her husband where he was taking up more than half the couch, his arms and legs spread out to the side. Casual, relaxed, at-home. Not looking like someone who'd just said what he had.

"What?"

"He needs a brother. You don't want him to be an only child, do you?"

"No…but when are you thinking he needs a brother?"

"Soon."

Ava laughed. "Says the man who didn't push this through his narrow hips." She gestured to Remy. "How soon?"

His brows plucked together. "I thought you wanted more." He sounded almost hurt, and it was adorable.

"I do. Of course I do. But not now. We don't want two in diapers, do we?"

"I don't…guess."

She bit back another laugh. "Merc, why do you look like I told you I'm gonna withhold sex for the next two weeks?"

"First off, you'd never do that, you can't resist," he said in all seriousness. Then he rubbed at his jaw and stared at the baby. "I dunno. I just…" He shrugged.

123

Poor baby, she thought. Coming to grips with his own bloodline had rattled him, and in typical Mercy fashion, he wanted to drown those worries in this new family he was making for himself.

"Life's short," he mused, one hand going to his bad knee. "You can be really practical and careful" – his eyes flicked to hers – "or you can do exactly what you want." He twitched a small, wry smile. "I wasted five years not doing what I wanted, *fillette*. I don't wanna waste our time anymore."

How could she argue with that? He wanted kids – and he was the perfect strong, tall, tree of a man that kids loved to climb. She didn't doubt, for a second, that no matter how many they had, he'd throw himself wholeheartedly into fatherhood, co-parenting with her. He didn't shrink from diapers, from spit-up, from middle-of-the-night screaming.

"You're the best daddy," she told him quietly, and his smile twitched. He blinked. "If you–"

Her phone rang and she stood, reaching for it in her back pocket before it could get Remy upset.

Her mom.

"Hey."

"Where are you?" Maggie's voice quivered with panic and emotion.

Ava's lungs seized up. "At home. Why?"

"Your bother – there was…Aidan took a fall." She sucked in a ragged breath that was like claws scraping across Ava's ear. "It's bad…Ava, it's bad. The blood–"

"I'm on my way," Ava said.

She was the only one in the family who shared his blood type.

She punched disconnect and turned to Mercy. He was already up off the couch, sensing the distress in her.

"Aidan crashed." Her voice sounded faraway in her ears.

"Shit. Where? How bad?"

"Bad. He…I gotta go."

They both whirled at the sound of a bike roaring up into the driveway. Mercy was already moving toward the door when someone started pounding on it.

It was Tango, breathless, his blue eyes saucer-wide in a blanched face. "Did you hear?"

"Mom just called." Ava needed shoes. Where the fuck were her shoes? "I'm on my way."

"Come on, I'll take you."

She located her boots and stepped into them without socks.

"Go with Tango," Mercy said, and she could tell he was being calm for her sake. "I'll get Remy's stuff together and head that way. I'll see you there in a bit."

"Okay." She pressed a fast kiss to his lips and snatched her helmet off its peg by the door. "Let's go."

Her hands were shaking wildly as she crammed her helmet down on her head, following Tango down the front sidewalk. She fumbled with the buckle, tripped over a crack in the concrete.

Tango swung a leg over his Harley, started it with a growl, and reached for her, pulling her snugly against his back on the bitch seat, ensuring her arms were wrapped tight around him, hands linked against his stomach before he took off.

She'd forgotten her sunglasses and closed her eyes tight against the sting of the wind, dropping her forehead onto Tango's shoulder, nose pressed against the sun-warmed leather of his cut. The cow hide had a way of retaining scents, and the usual clubhouse smells tunneled up her nostrils: smoke, beer, brake dust, motor oil…and something else. A cologne she didn't recognize, embedded deep into the skin.

Tango's stomach trembled under her palms, and she'd ridden behind these guys enough times to know vibration – versus the leaping of muscles. He was quivering, shaking all over.

He was as much Aidan's sibling as she was.

This was what it had been like for Aidan, she figured. That afternoon in New Orleans, when the club van had pulled up and found the carnage, when Mercy had been pinned beneath his bike and she'd been clutching an empty gun, three dead at her feet – this was the crippling shock and panic her brother had felt then. But Aidan had pushed through it; he'd leapt to action.

Just as she was going to.

Tango pulled his bike up in a loading zone and they abandoned it in a mad rush, heedless of the cop yelling that they couldn't park there. The automatic doors slid wide, chilled, hospital-smelling air enveloping them as they bolted inside. Mild, sweet-natured Tango shoved people aside as they went through the ER toward the desk.

"Aidan Teague," Ava said with a gasp as her hands slapped down on the counter. "Bike crash. He came in–" deep inhale, struggling for breath – "about fifteen minutes–"

"Are you the sister?" the nurse asked.

She nodded.

"Follow me."

It stretched into one of those permanent moments, the ones that lodged like grit in her mind to be bathed into a pearl, remembered forever after in flawless detail. The long hurried walk down the hall, Tango panting behind her, the nurse's Crocs squeaking on the tile ahead of her. Half-closed drapes and glimpses of people behind them, wrapped in bandages, clutching at wounds, softly crying into tissues. Smell of antiseptic and blood. Murmur of voices and electric chatter of life-sustaining equipment.

They were led not to Aidan, but to an empty bed. The nurse pushed the curtain wide and said, "Hop up on the bed and someone will be in in a minute to draw."

Ava nodded, complying in a rush, as if that might somehow bring the tech along faster with the needle and the empty pint bag. She turned her hand palm-up on her thigh and then curled it into a fist, watching the blue-green vein in the crook of her elbow jump and darken.

Come on, come on…

She'd seen terrible bike crashes. She didn't have to imagine what her brother looked like now.

She lifted her head, question on her lips…and saw that Tango was in much worse shape than she was. He was white to his hairline, and his lips pressed together and then smoothed as if he were trying to force himself to be calm; twitching. He clutched at the plastic foot of the bed with both hands, knuckles white and knobby, the dominoes on the backs of his fingers stark by contrast. The veins stood out in his thin arms.

Ava swallowed the lump in her throat. Tried to. "How'd it happen?"

He shook his head. "A car clipped him from behind. He…" He drew in a shattered breath, eyes glossy with moisture. "He went under it."

"Jesus," she whispered, heart lurching against her ribs.

"Dublin's gonna pick up the bike. What's left of it." He lifted one hand and wiped it across his eyes, face scrunching up. "Jesus," he echoed her whisper. "Oh, Jesus Christ."

Ava leaned over and grabbed at his hand where it rested on the bed, covering his rigid fingers with her own. "He'll be okay. Aidan's too ornery to go out like this."

But the words had a hollow ring, and neither of them were going to acknowledge it.

He bowed his head over hers, struggling to regain his composure with deep, shuddering breaths that stirred the hair on the top of her head.

The clacking of plastic wheels announced the arrival of a tech with a cart and Tango stepped back, turning away from her, wiping at his face some more.

"Okay," the tech – brawny young guy who might have looked comical in his green scrubs if the situation hadn't been so grave – snapped on gloves. "This is for" – consult of the screen on the cart – "Aidan Teague?"

"Yes, I'm his sister." Ava reached out her arm for the compression band he would tie to it. "Take as much as you need; I'm his blood type."

"Eat your cookie." Thinking about the fact that Ava was about to pass out kept him from thinking quite so much about his best friend laid open on the operating table like a broken toy. The way she was listing hard against him, frowning at the chocolate chip bakery cookie a nurse had brought her along with a cup of juice, was something he could fix. He had no medical powers, could only wait helpless like the rest of them, but he could do something about Ava's impending swoon.

She took a reluctant bite and chewed like it was cardboard. It smelled delicious, and that made Tango want to barf.

Or maybe that was just the terror cycling through him.

Ava had only been able to donate a pint. Glassy-eyed, weaving so badly he'd had to hold her around the waist afterward as they walked, she'd insisted they take more.

"She's nursing a baby," Tango had told the tech, half-worried her insistence would persuade the guy.

But the man in the green scrubs had shaken his head. "We can't take any more than this. She's too little."

"And drink your juice," he added. He didn't care if her mom was in the chair across from them, he was going to make sure she didn't pass out. He could do that. He could help in that way.

They were in a small family waiting room on the surgical floor. Maggie looked numb, the way she stared at the fire escape route taped above their heads, but her eyes were the giveaway, the gateways to the frenzy of her heart inside her composed outer shell.

Ghost couldn't sit still; he paced, hands on his hips, glancing darkly toward the doors every so often, bristling at every sound from the hallway. What if it was bad news the doctor brought? Tango

127

wondered – would he finally see the man lose it? A real, honest to God breakdown?

Carter was slouched in the chair on the other side of Ava, and he'd run his hands through his hair so many times it stood out at quirky angles from his head.

They waited. And they waited.

Mercy appeared in the entrance, coming in from the hall, Remy's carrier in one hand. At a different time, Tango would have laughed to see the fiercest-looking man he knew holding a baby in a white plastic seat, but now he only nodded in greeting.

"Any word?" he asked.

"Nah." Ghost shook his head and patted the guy on the shoulder.

"He'll be in surgery for a while," Maggie said, and Mercy leaned down so she could kiss his cheek. Then he held the baby up in his carrier so she could greet her grandson.

Carter stood and slid down a seat, giving Mercy room to sit down next to his old lady.

Tango was sorry to lose the warmth of her shoulder as she shifted over stiffly like a metronome so she could lean against her husband. He wanted to be touching someone right now. He wanted someone's weight against him, to counterbalance the awful weight of guilt.

"You're supposed to eat that, you know," Mercy said.

Ava made a face and took another laborious bite of cookie.

He murmured something to her in French, some little endearment meant only for her.

Tango let his head fall back until it touched the wall. His chest ached, and his head throbbed. He hadn't been at the shop when the call came in. He'd arrived at Dartmoor to find the place in a panic. Carter had only been half through his explanation of what was happening before Tango was on his bike. Blood loss meant blood transfusion. Blood meant Ava, the only relative who shared his type. Half-sister to the rescue, and he would have mown anyone down who dared to slow their progress.

I should have been there, he thought over and over. *I should have been with him when it happened.* Maybe, if they'd been riding together, he could have seen the car; could have put his bike between, could have suggested they stop for smokes and delayed the fortuitous meeting on the street of biker and Mustang.

He hadn't been riding alongside his best friend because he'd taken another of those goddamn long lunches. A lunch that, unlike the three-way romp with Jazz and the psycho, was completely inexcusable, under any circumstances. A lunch that involved expensive brandy, real Cuban cigars, butter-soft leather furniture and the unwelcome lullaby effect of that polite English voice he had known so well before – and now knew again, in this new capacity. The capacity that made him a traitor to the club for fraternizing with a potential enemy. Whatever Shaman was to the Lean Dogs, he wasn't a friend. But Tango tried to convince himself that wandering down memory lane with his old friend Ian had nothing to do with the Dogs, or Shaman, or anything.

Then why was he keeping it secret?

And why did he want to drag a razor across his wrist right now?

The sound of the doors opening jerked him upright. The doctor who entered the waiting room had tiny spots of blood peppering the sleeves of his surgical gown.

"Just wanted to give you an update."

Tango could feel the strain in the room, the painful waiting of all of them.

"Doctor Miller has stopped all the bleeding, and Aidan has stabilized. We're going to begin repairs now."

"Thank you," Maggie said, speaking for all of them.

Tango slumped back against the wall, and inside, the guilt raged.

Maggie didn't want coffee. She wanted three fingers of whiskey with two ice cubes, in the fat-bottomed tumbler from the upper right shelf of the cabinet above the microwave at home. But she said, "Thanks," and took the steaming foam cup from the hair-net-wearing employee on the other side of the hospital cafeteria counter.

The word *cafeteria* conjured the scent of bleach and the squeak of kids' sneakers; the sterile white cinderblock and linoleum confines of a middle school, greasy steaming food slopped onto plastic trays. But this was more of a bistro, the rich color palette and café tables detracting from the buffet line and the hair nets. It smelled a hell of a lot better than a school cafeteria too: garlic, basil, turmeric, frying onions and peppers.

She took her cup over to the condiment station and added sugar and cream; her hand shook and she dropped the plastic cream cup twice. She stirred it and blew the steam off the top, though she had no intention of drinking it. This was how she coped; the preservation of normalcy in the face of disaster was the best thing she'd taken away from her mother, and she used it in moments like these. Moments when the stepson who was more like a brother to her was dying on an operating table…

Ghost was waiting for her when she turned around, arms folded across his chest, brows drawn as he surveyed the cafeteria like he was on guard duty.

He jerked a little when she laid her hand on his arm.

"You should get something," she said. "Some coffee or–"

"I'm good."

She sighed. "Well no, actually, you're not, baby." She sifted her fingertips through the dark hair on his arm. "You're shaking."

He shook his head in denial, but said nothing.

She leaned in close to him, the steam from her cup slithering up between them. "Of all the things he's quit," she whispered, "he likes being alive too much to quit life. He's going to be *fine*, Kenny."

He swallowed hard, his Adam's apple working.

It wasn't just terror running in tremors beneath his skin. She could feel the guilt there, too. Guilt because he was a cold father, without tenderness and grace when it came to his children, and as much as he hated that about himself, he couldn't seem to change it. And this was the nightmare – his firstborn dying and never knowing there was love there.

"It's time," she said, patting his forearm, tone that of gentle reprimand. "When he's out of here, and he's better, it's time you start teaching him to be a man. You both need that."

His eyes looked black and harsh when they slid to her face. "No one had to teach me."

"He's not you," she countered. "And that's okay."

He put both arms around her and held her tight against his chest.

Mercy wanted to hate hospitals. Most days, he did. He never seemed to be within the walls of one for a happy reason. Someone had wrecked, someone had been attacked, someone was old and sick, someone needed surgery.

But there had been that one time.

"You're not gonna go *in there*, are you?" Aidan had asked, nose wrinkled in a boyish display of disgust.

Mercy hadn't bothered to answer him. There may have been boundaries and rules between mature, collected adults who'd married one another based on some sequence of compatibility tests. But his *fillette* was having his baby – wild horses, and all that.

He'd seen women on TV melting like candles under the onslaught of pain, strain, and heat. Ava's skin was flushed and damp, but there was no melting. Loose strands of dark hair clung to the back of her neck, to her temples. She breathed through her teeth and the look on her face was the fiercest determination he'd ever witnessed.

"He's a big one," Dr. Wyatt said. "This is going to hurt, Ava, but I need you to push *hard.*" He looked at Mercy, up at her head. "Dad, you want to give her something to brace against?"

He looped his arm around her knee and leaned low into her; he could feel her breath against his face, smell her sweat, and fear, and purpose. In French he told her how strong she was, and that she could do this, not to worry.

A nurse gave her a bracing hand for her other foot, and then it was all up to her. He couldn't do this for her, though he wanted to take the burden.

But of course she didn't need that burden lifted. She had this.

Being pressed against her as she brought their son into the world was the most terrifying and magnificent moment of his life. And then there was Remy, all slimy and skinny and screaming.

"Good strong lungs," Dr. Wyatt had said with a smile, and put the baby up on Ava's stomach, let her see and touch him a moment before the cord was cut.

She'd burst into gut-wrenching sobs, fingertips skimming across his mucus-covered skull. "He's here," she'd whispered. "He's here, he's here, he's really here."

His little eyes were moving now, as he lay in his carrier, fingers curling in the air, gaze taking in the waiting room with astonishing alertness. Mercy had expected babies to just sit like lumps and not engage. He hadn't expected this intense absorption, the way Remy's eyes came to their faces when they spoke, the way he noticed every sound and movement.

Ava was leaning into his shoulder, letting him hold more of his weight than she should have.

"Did you eat your cookie?" he asked, turning his head so her hair pressed up under his nose.

"Working on it." It was a big cookie, one of those nice ones from the bakery in the cafeteria, and she'd nibbled about half of it away.

"Juice?"

She tipped her empty cup toward him so he could see the last clinging drops of orange juice at the bottom.

Mercy let his lips linger against the shiny smoothness of her hair, an almost-kiss. "I'm kinda glad, you know?"

She made an inquisitive sound around another bite of cookie.

"Now I won't be the only gimp in the family."

She elbowed him hard, and he smiled. She wasn't feeling *that* weak.

Ghost and Maggie returned from their trip downstairs, Maggie with a coffee cup, both of them with shadows in their eyes. Ghost's jaw was clenched so tight, it would crack if he sneezed.

"Anyone been by?" Maggie asked, a hopeful note threaded through her voice.

"No," Tango and Carter said together, miserable.

She sighed –

And then the double doors that led into the sinister interior of the hospital opened and the doctor was back.

Mercy felt Ava go rigid against his side.

Tango sat upright, looking electrified.

The doctor surveyed them…and smiled.

Thirteen
Half-Measures

Aidan had only pretended to be sick once in his life; and that was only because he'd been able to pull it off once. After that, Mags got wise (wis*er*), and he was never able to fake it after that. That one day, she'd been too late for work to do more than press her hand to his head, find the skin hot and dry from his efforts with the hair dryer, then throw meds and an *I love you* his way before rushing out the door. He'd spent the entire day in front of the TV, raiding the fridge, stuffing himself with ice cream and pizza pockets until he was sick. It had been bliss – nothing to do but sit and vegetate.

He'd learned in the last few weeks that doing nothing was only fun when you were lounging by choice. Being bedridden because a yellow goddamn muscle car had run over you sucked ass.

Miraculous. That's what the doctor's had said. It was a miracle the car had gone over his arm, and not his center of mass. His helmet had saved his life. It had been touch-and-go after surgery, the worry that the internal repairs and patches wouldn't hold, and that he'd start to bleed again. But it had been miraculous, all things considered, and he would eventually make a full recovery.

But what about his ink?

He'd been wearing a t-shirt beneath his cut that evening, and when he'd rolled end over end across the pavement, the asphalt had abraded his bare arms; had sanded off the top layer of skin. The subdermal ink looked jagged and irregular beneath the thick crusty scabs all down his forearms. Thank God the sleeves had protected his shoulders. His roses.

The TV was on, but he was watching a cable showing of *The Dark Knight* and the screen was mostly dark, giving him a nice glimpse of his sad-sack sorry self all bundled up in Ava's guest bed, head tipped back against the headboard, throat knobby, skinny, and nothing like the way he remembered.

He'd lost twenty pounds during all this.

He looked like shit and didn't feel much better than that.

A light rap at the door preceded Ava's entrance. She slipped in quickly and quietly, like a thin shadow in black tank top and skinny jeans.

"Need anything before I go?"

He needed a lot of things, none of which his sister could provide. She'd been outstanding, he had to give her credit: when he was released from the hospital, it had been apparent to all of them that he couldn't bunk at the clubhouse or go home to the apartment. Ava didn't start school until late August, so she'd volunteered the spare bedroom at her house. She and Mags had both looked after him that first week, but without Ava and Mercy – well, he didn't like to think about not having their help.

Ava had brought him his pills at the right times and ensured he took them. She'd kept him hydrated, fed him when he could choke stuff down, kept Chapstick and water, magazines and chocolate on the bedside table. In the evenings, Mercy had hooked an ungodly strong arm around his waist and helped him shower. Had washed his hair like he was an infant. *This must be how he is with Remy*, Aidan had reflected beneath the coursing hot water. That giant hand so gentle as it curved around his skull, working flower-smelling shampoo into his hair.

They had served as siblings, parents, and hospital staff, never complaining, never acting like he was a burden.

Through the walls, at night, when the pain meds weren't strong enough to send him to sleep, he lay in a fuzzy trance and listened to their murmured voices. The low chatter of in-depth conversation. The smoky Cajun rumble of Mercy's chuckle. Ava's high, bright laugher. He heard the baby fuss and heard them go to him down the hall. He heard their bed creak and listened to those timeless, unmistakable sounds he'd heard so often on the other side of closed dorm doors; there was a difference in pitch with them, though, something sweet and warm, rather than the desperation he was so used to.

They were this little family unto themselves, wanting nothing, but acting glad to have him.

Ava was going back to school this afternoon. Just one class, from two to four, and then she'd pick Remy up from Mags at Dartmoor and be back.

Aidan was terrified.

He dampened his lips. "I…" What did he want? For his baby sister to sit home with him? He couldn't say that. So he said, "Nah, I'm good," staring at the TV so she wouldn't see the pleading in his eyes.

What a pussy.

She hesitated a moment. "I made you lunch. I'll bring that and some more Gatorade. Okay?"

" 'Kay."

**

134

Because she'd called ahead, Sam found the back door of the Lécuyer house unlocked when she arrived. She let herself in, turned the deadbolt behind her, and walked into the kitchen in search of Ava.

There was a wooden tray perched on the table holding someone's lunch. Ava stood at the fridge, putting a casserole dish away on the shelf. Remy was crying in his swing on the floor.

"Remy, Remy, Remy," Ava said as she pushed the fridge door shut with her hip. To Sam: "I'm sorry, I'm ready to go, but I'm gonna have to change him first."

"That's fine." Sam hooked her purse on the back of a chair. "No rush."

They'd decided to carpool today, since it was the first day, and since parking would be such a nightmare. After the first week of class, the dropouts and the class-skippers would stop coming to class, and the lots would be thinned. But for today, they were taking Ava's truck together. In case they had to park in a median.

"Great. Sorry," Ava said again, bending over the swing and unhooking Remy's straps. "Oh, hey, would you mind running that tray back to my brother? I told him I'd bring him lunch before I left."

Just like that, there was a fist tightening around her stomach.

Sam swallowed, throat suddenly dry, gorge suddenly rising. All those old physical manifestations of nerves. Aidan Teague – who she had lusted over, been morose over, who hadn't remembered her – would surely remember their last run-in, when she'd called him a jackass and cut him down hard. She didn't want him. The last of her romantic notions had been blasted to bits by his forgetfulness. But she wasn't keen on being in the same room with him after their last awkward encounter.

And then she remembered that he'd nearly died in a motorcycle crash, and shame heated her cheeks.

"Sure." She picked up the tray. "The second bedroom?"

"Uh-huh." Ava was already headed into the living room with Remy and the diaper bag.

Sam took a deep, steadying breath, and went down the hall.

Ava was by no means a chef, but her cooking had improved just in the time that Sam had known her. On the tray for Aidan's lunch she'd put together a club sandwich packed with cold cuts and real skillet-fried bacon, lettuce, tomato, mustard dribbling down the sides. Instead of chips there were sweet potato fries. A bowl of steamed broccoli. A small dessert plate with a fat chocolate chip brownie. And two white pills beside the Coke: his pain meds.

The bedroom door was ajar and on the other side of it she could hear the dim rumble of the TV. She hesitated a moment, unsure what to expect. Then she eased the door open with her elbow and stepped in.

It was a small spare bedroom, but there was room for a double bed against one wall, and a low-slung bureau across from it that held the TV. The bedside table was covered with water and Gatorade bottles, prescription bottles, magazines, scraps of tissue, a Dove chocolates sampler. On either side of the TV, the bureau was loaded with nasal spray, eye drops, body lotion, boxes of gauze, bandages and bottles of antiseptic. The blinds were open, but with the sun so high overhead, the light stayed on the other side of the window, almost as if it were afraid to pierce the gloom with even the thinnest fingers. The room smelled like rubbing alcohol, and clammy sheets, and illness.

And there was Aidan, propped up on a stack of pillows against the headboard, head tipped back like it was too heavy to hold up, his left arm in a cast and sling.

For the first time, she understood the true meaning of the phrase "death warmed over."

The weight loss was the most shocking part, the way he was all angles, his t-shirt too loose, his features startling in this new, narrower face. His glossy curly hair was dull. The right arm, the one that hadn't been run over, was a mess of cracked dark scabs, all the vivid ink hidden beneath them. When she first stepped in, his eyes were closed, and the flesh around them looked dark, bruised.

She was struck suddenly by the knowledge that she'd never seen her father after his accident. The one that had killed him. Her mother had identified the body at the morgue while Sam was at work, and she'd only seen him later, when the funeral home had dressed and made him up for the viewing. He'd looked almost alive then. It was amazing what they could do with cosmetics.

He'd looked more alive than Aidan did now.

Her hands started to shake, and the plates clicked together on the tray.

Aidan's eyes opened and slid toward her, brows drawing low when he saw that she wasn't his sister.

"Ava needed to change the baby before we left," she explained, "and she asked me to bring you this."

He stared at her one long, unreadable moment, then his eyes went to the TV. " 'Kay. Thanks."

Was he unhappy to see her? Or was this simply about his condition? His truly awful condition.

136

The tray was the kind intended to go over a lap, so she stepped up to the bed and set the tray carefully over the shapes of his legs beneath the covers.

"You don't have to—" he protested, hitching himself up higher against the headboard.

"It's no problem." She made sure the tray was stable and not about to tip over, and then she straightened, not wanting to linger in his personal space. She wasn't his family or his friend.

He cleared his throat as he stared down at the food. "I'm not all that hungry."

"Maybe you will be when you start eating," she suggested.

No comment.

"You probably shouldn't take those pills on an empty stomach." What the hell was she doing? Just get out of the room!

A frown twitched at the corners of his mouth. "Won't matter. Not like I can operate heavy machinery or anything."

"It might upset your stomach."

"I've got a trash can to puke in."

He was lifeless. And it was heartbreaking.

The contrast between the swaggering, cocky bastard who'd walked into Ava's kitchen a week ago and this dull shadow of a man stirred a strange ache inside her. Aidan may have been indifferent, and cruel in the way that all beautiful men were cruel – but to see him laid so low brought her no pleasure.

"I think you should eat," she said, recognizing her tone as the cajoling one she always used with her sister. "You'll feel better."

He looked toward her again, and she thought, for a second, that he almost smiled. "What do you care if a jackass feels better?"

She pressed her lips together to keep from groaning, her face heating. "That was a regrettable choice of words."

"Regrettable." His derisive snort sounded tired, a shade of his usual attitude. "You sound like my sister."

She was grateful for the sudden prickling of irritation; it eased her guilt. "That's probably why we're friends. We're both writers."

"Right." He let his head flop back onto the pillow but was still holding eye contact. "I don't get that. Why would anybody wanna spend all that time writing stuff down?"

It sounded curious, rather than caustic.

Sam shrugged and folded her arms. "It's not really something you wake up one day and choose to do. It's a calling. It sings to you, and you have to answer."

A thoughtful face from him that was worlds more attractive than all his venomous snark.

"What about you?" she asked. "Doesn't the open road call to you, or something like that?" Humorless chuckle. "Because why would anybody wanna spend all that time picking bugs out of his teeth?"

He grinned, and despite the pallor and the thinness, the expression transformed his face, revived him a little. "Alright, fair play." He shifted, and then he looked more comfortable, more relaxed. His eyes came to her face and stayed there, longer than she would have liked, long enough to make her want to squirm inside her clothes.

"You were really quiet," Aidan said after a while. "And you always wore that huge sweater. And your glasses were round instead of that shape." He gestured toward the chic rectangular frames that perched on top of her nose.

Sam nodded, and felt her pulse flutter, a small beating of wings at the base of her throat. "Yeah."

Thoughtful face again. "You grew up." And the phrase meant so many things all at once, she didn't know which to latch onto. "I didn't recognize you the other day, honest to God. I wasn't trying to be a dick."

She managed a faint smile. "You do it so well though."

When he laughed it sounded like it hurt his chest, the low rattle deep beneath his ribs.

The softening she felt was dangerous. She did not need to allow herself to feel tenderness and sympathy for this man...and yet she couldn't help it. He was beyond pathetic right now.

And he'd remembered her after all.

"Do you need anything else before we leave?" she asked, and hated the way she sounded worried. Hated it a little, anyway.

"Nah, I'm good." He sounded surer of himself now. "Most days I can go take a leak by myself." When she didn't respond, he said, "I'm kidding. I can at least do *that*." His eyes skittered away, though, like maybe a day or so ago, he'd needed help with that most basic human function.

"We won't be gone that long."

"It's fine. Go. Be nerds. Write shit." He gave her another of those almost-normal grins. "Sing back to it, or whatever the hell."

She smiled. "Wow. That was poetic. You sure you don't want to come?"

He shuddered dramatically. "There's a reason I never got my GED."

Yes, and a stupid one at that.

"Okay." She needed to take a step back, but didn't. Not yet. "I'll…see you later then. Eat your lunch, if you can."

His gaze dropped to his plate. "Yeah. Ava doesn't turn everything into an old shoe anymore. It's eatable."

Edible, she corrected silently in her head.

"Sam!" Ava called from down the hall. "I'm done with the baby."

Really no reason to linger any longer.

"I should go," she said, and turned for the door.

"See ya," Aidan said behind her, and she heard the plates clinking around as he contemplated his food.

And then he added, "Sam."

As it turned out, he wasn't alone for very long.

The problem with eating was, it sounded terrible, until he actually started eating. And then he realized he was starving. And sometimes, he bolted his food like a hungry chocolate Lab and then puked it all back up. So he'd learned his lesson. The club sandwich turned out to be exactly what he wanted, but he made himself take it slow, small dainty bites like he was some kind of goddamn princess, and was more than halfway through when he heard a bike outside. He knew all his brothers' bikes, because he'd done most of the work on them. A clear audio of the ringing tailpipes, and he could place each bike and each Dog.

This was Tango.

For ease of visiting during his recovery, Ava had hidden a key under a broken flowerpot by the back door, so visitors could come and go if she wasn't at home. Aidan listened to the bike shut off; to the scrape of the key in the lock, the door opening and closing, Tango's light, ballerina footfalls as he moved through the house.

"Hey," his voice said on the other side of the door before it was pushed inward.

"Hey," Aidan echoed, slammed again by the shame he felt each time one of his club brothers saw him in this bed.

Tango left the door open as he stepped into the room and dropped into the recliner Mercy had set up beside the dresser. It was a ratty, hand-me-down thing, angled toward the bed. His first few nights at home, Ava had slept there, watching over him, worrying, being better than a half-sister had ever been in the history of half-sisters.

"Lunch?" Tango asked.

"You look like you could use it more than me."

Tango shrugged. He'd always been thin; he had one of those long, slender physiques. A dancer's build, Maggie had called it, before she knew the horrible ironic truth of the words. But now, today, he looked the thinnest Aidan had ever seen him. Skinny like when he'd finally broken away from his old profession and he'd still had veins choked with heroin. The baggy clothes could only hide it so well. He was like a scarecrow beneath his t-shirt. Everything about the graceful way he walked was hidden inside the wide legs of his jeans.

"You look like shit, man," Aidan said.

"Coming from you, that *is* an insult."

"Hey, I was a douchebag's hood ornament. What's your excuse?"

Tango attempted a smile…but it got the best of him, and he wound up studying the dominoes on his fingers, chewing at the inside of his cheek.

"Bro, what's wrong?"

He shook his head. "Nothing. Just tired."

"It's hot as hell outside; everyone's tired."

Tango stretched out his hand, turned it over, held it to the light. His fingers were skinny as matchsticks, and looked just as brittle. He'd brought a heaviness into the room with him; there was something he wanted to say, but he couldn't bring himself to do so yet.

"How's Jazz doing?" Aidan asked, to change the subject.

Going by the way Tango's brow crimped, Jazz was somehow a part of the burden. "She's good," he said, curling his hand into a fist and tucking it into his lap alongside the other one.

"The bruises are gone, yeah?" Aidan prodded.

"Yeah, for a while now. She's alright. She's kinda jumpy when somebody walks up behind her."

"Gettin' strangled'll do that."

"Yeah."

"She's not still trying to set you up with anybody is she?"

Tango shook his head. "No. I think she…I think she figured out that wasn't ever going to work."

"It could work."

Tango shot him a withering glance. "How?"

Aidan shrugged and almost tipped his lunch tray over. He grabbed at it with one hand and gestured vaguely with the other. "I dunno—"

"You're not exactly the one to be giving advice on that front."

"Hey, I never said I was." He scowled. "But you could…shit, you could try to meet somebody. A real chick, and not a groupie. And, maybe…ease her into things slow."

"What things? The club? The tats? Or the fact that I got–"

"You only tell her what you want to!" Aidan was too tired and weak not to be exasperated "Do you think the guys in this club are totally honest with their old ladies?"

Tango's blue eyes glimmered with emotion; anger tightened his jaw until the cords in his neck stood out. "Some of them are."

Aidan snorted. "Sorry I don't have another sister for you to hook up with."

Tango gathered himself, tightening all over, like he was preparing to stand, but all he did was turn his head away. When he swallowed, the movement of his throat looked painful.

"Shit." Aidan sighed. "Kev, you know that all of us – that Dad, and Mags, and Ava and Merc and me – know what happened to you. And we don't care, and we love you. You've got us." He leaned forward, not caring that his brownie slid off the plate onto the blanket. "*You've got us.*"

Another big, painful, throat-jerking swallow.

"But I think, for you, we're not enough," he added as gently as he could, because he didn't mean it as an insult. "I think you need something we can't give you."

"You make it sound like there's something wrong with me."

"There is. You're sad as fuck all the time lately."

Tango dropped his forehead into his hand. His pale lashes flickered as he blinked. "I'm sorry."

"You don't gotta be sorry about it."

"No…I'm sorry I wasn't there," he said against his wrist. "The day you crashed, I shoulda been there. I shoulda been with you. But I was–" He drew in a shallow, ragged breath. "Jesus," he whispered. "I'm sorry. I was–"

"Ian," Aidan said grimly, and knew it was true when Tango didn't respond. "You went to see him, didn't you?"

Silence was his answer.

"Damn it, man. Why? Why would you do that to yourself?"

Tango shook his head. "We've just had lunch a few times. Just…not as Tango and Shaman. It's got nothing to do with the club and his business."

"That doesn't answer the question, dude. *Why do that to yourself?*"

"I can handle it," he said, swallowing hard, lifting his head with a resolute expression. "It's just lunch. Talking and shit. And really good wine. I'm not *doing anything to myself.*"

"Bullshit. That guy's poison. Being around him is like opening up all your old shit. He'll bleed all over you."

"No."

Aidan sighed through his nose, deeply frustrated. "You get what he's doing, right? He's using you. He's getting you all stuck in the past, and he's going to try to get club intel out of you. Fuck," he muttered, angrier the more he talked. "He's trying to turn you into a goddamn mole, Kev!"

"He's not."

"News flash – that's what enemies do."

"He's not my enemy," Tango said quietly.

Aidan sat back hard against the headboard. "Shit."

"When it comes to the club, yeah, Shaman's probably gonna be a problem. But to me? He's Ian. My friend Ian from way back in the day. The only one who kept me sane during–" His jaw tightened, not willing to say it.

"I was there too," Aidan said, frowning. "All through high school."

"Yeah, you were. But you were on the outside of…that part of my life."

"Oh, what. You miss it or something?"

"Never," he said emphatically. "But I can't pretend it didn't happen. And I can't pretend Ian is just some businessman."

"You're stuck in the past."

"The past is complicated."

"Shit," Aidan repeated, letting his head fall back until it thunked against the headboard. "Dad would go ape shit if he knew you were having fucking brandy and cigars with that guy."

A nervous tension crept into Tango's voice. "Are you gonna tell him?"

Aidan shut his eyes. "Never." He echoed his friend's conviction.

It was silent a long tense beat. Two…three…

"I wish he hadn't come back to Knoxville."

"I know," Aidan said, the tightness in his chest loosening. Kev worked so hard to forget that he'd been owned by someone once, that he'd been addicted to heroin and made to perform for the entire first half of his life.

"But he did."

"He did." And a man wasn't likely to forget the sole friend who'd walked side-by-side with him through that awful dark underground world.

Even if he was toxic.

Even if he had new friends now.

Some past events just refused to fade into memory.

"It's okay," Aidan told him, eyes still shut. "I won't tell anyone."

And I won't let you get sucked back into the void, he added silently.

Fourteen
Dad Talk

"You've been exercising?" Maggie asked as she cleared empty water bottles into the trash bag she carried. She'd brought an empty Hefty sack in with her and was moving methodically around the room, loading it with empty McDonald's cups, napkins, bits of receipts, various whatnot that left her lip curled up in maternal disgust.

He sighed and swung his legs up onto the bed in a sequence of smooth movements that were habit by this point. "Down the hall and back twice this morning."

"I think you should increase it."

"The doc said—"

"That once we moved past the dangerous time with your neck, it would good to start working back toward a modified daily workout routine." She gave him a pointed look. "I was there for that conversation, remember?"

Aidan ground his molars together and said nothing. A fraction, that's what the doctor had said. If his neck had twisted one fraction more, it would have snapped, and he wouldn't be here littering Ava's spare bedroom right now.

The bruising, swelling, general inflammation, the strain, the severely misaligned vertebrae – it wouldn't heal up in a snap of the fingers. He was looking at a long road to his promised full recovery. But he was on the mend. Simply getting out of bed was no longer a major worry. He didn't need Mercy to wash his hair anymore, thank God.

But he was afraid.

And he didn't want to admit that to anyone.

"Yeah," he muttered, letting his head fall back against the high-stacked pillows. It felt better to take the strain off, mimic the natural curve of his neck like this, stretch those little-used muscles.

He heard a bike in the driveway. Damn, that sound was getting old. He was supposed to be the one out there in the driveway, not the sad piece of shit in here listening to Lean Dogs come and go.

Maggie pulled out the ties on the bag and set them in a tidy knot. "That'll be your dad," she said, and as Aidan swore quietly to himself, she added, "just hear what he has to say. I think you two need some father/son time, and you're a captive audience, so to speak." Her smile started out amused, then became soft and genuine. "He was so worried about you. In the hospital" – her lower lip trembled the slightest – "just try to remember, no matter what he ever says to you, no matter how grouchy he is – he loves you so much."

He rolled his eyes as she turned her back. "Okay?"

"If you say so."

She set the bag in the hall, then came back and kissed his forehead. "Love you."

"You too."

Then she was gone, rustling sound of the Hefty bag following her as she dragged it down the hall.

He listened to Ghost enter; heard the two of them exchange words he couldn't make out. Then the back door opened, closed, and Maggie's Caddy started with a low purr a moment later.

Ghost's boots sounded heavy and mean as he moved through the kitchen. Then he toed them off. *Thunk. Thunk.* And his socked feet came down the hall toward the bedroom.

Normal, everyday sounds, no different than Mercy shedding boots and cut and coming back here to deliver the day's mail and gossip.

But his gut writhed.

Ghost let the door swing all the way open – a quick push with his fingertips – before he stepped into the room. He was wearing an ancient faded Gilley's t-shirt he'd picked up on a Texas run years ago. He'd brought shirts for Aidan, too, none of which he could wear anymore; he'd passed them down to Ava when he outgrew them.

Maggie's words echoed in his head. *"He loves you so much."*

Did he really? Was that love? T-shirts?

Over the silkscreen mechanical bull on his shirt, Ghost's cut looked heavy, burdened with that president patch.

"Hey," he said, arms folding, taking up a spot against the closet door.

"Hey."

"You look better." His mouth twitched in a quick, sideways smile that was identical to the one Aidan flashed himself in the mirror most days. It was more a smirk, really; it felt sinister coming from his father, for reasons he didn't want to think about. "Like shit, but better."

"Feels the same. Shit, but better."

Ghost snorted. "Seeing as how you're not in a wheelchair, *shit* is pretty damn good."

"Yeah."

145

Awkward. This was awkward as hell.

Had it ever not been? Aidan tunneled back through his memories, searching for something light, warm, tender even. He knew there had to be moments like that, but hopped up on oxy, he couldn't bring them to mind.

"Tango said the shop was real busy," he said, searching for a safe topic.

Ghost nodded, seeming relieved. "Yeah, it's been good riding weather, so lots of bikes have been coming in. All the regulars, plus" – he chuckled – "had this whole RC come through last week, old ladies on the back. Buncha dentists or accountants or some shit, on a long weekend ride, and one of their Hondas was sputtering like an old cat. Had to send Carter out for a part, so the whole crew took up the parking lot for an hour. Wannabes," he said with disgust, but grinned. "This one shithead wanted to get chatty with Merc, compare bikes and shit."

Aidan grinned, envisioning it. "How'd Merc take it?"

"Oh, he ate it up. That guy and his wife left thinking he was a teddy bear."

"Yeah."

Ghost sobered. "I think we need to talk."

Shit. "About what?"

Ghost moved to sit on the foot of the bed. Shoulders slumped. Gaze fixed on Aidan's feet where they made lumps beneath the covers. "I think there's some things I took for granted that you already knew. Things you would...grow into with time."

His gaze lifted and it was stern, fatherly. Presidential. "The truth is, I've been worried about being your leader in the club, instead of your father."

No arguing with that. But hearing the words stirred up an old ache in Aidan's chest. "You were a shitty sponsor, too."

Ghost frowned – his automatic response – but then sighed. "Fair enough." He nodded. "I don't wanna talk about sponsor/prospect shit. Deal? No patches, no rank, just you and me."

"Okay."

And then it got quiet again.

Ghost's eyes dropped to his hands, the way the fingers of his right hand spun his wedding ring around. Aidan knew he couldn't get the thing off – not after fracturing that knuckle a few years ago in a fistfight – and that he wasn't bothered by that. He wouldn't have removed it anyway.

He lifted his head. "I know you were hoping to be nominated for VP last year, when Walsh got the nod."

Aidan blinked. He hadn't said anything, and frankly, with the Carpathians war and Mercy's accident, he hadn't expected Ghost to notice.

"You didn't have to say it; I could tell. And at the time, I thought you knew why I didn't put your name forward, but now I'm not sure."

"I wasn't ready," Aidan said woodenly.

"You're not, and you're not gonna be until you get your life figured out."

He felt his brows go up. "What?"

"The day you crashed." Ghost gave him his most unnerving level stare. "What were you doing?"

"I was going to check in with Fisher, like you asked me to."

"Yeah, but what were you doing when the crash happened?"

There was a snake twisting around in his belly.

"I pulled up on a scene that involves you, a yellow Mustang, a chick flashing too much cleavage and some asshole prick behind the wheel. You were racing." Not a question.

Aidan swallowed and said nothing.

"You were racing down the center of the city like a teenager, for the sheer hell of it, and you almost killed yourself." It was said not with censure, but with deep disappointment.

The little boy, though, Aidan said to himself. *I could have killed him, but I took the fall instead. I chose him over me.*

He'd chosen Greg over himself too, the day he hadn't been able to pull the trigger.

But Ghost didn't know about that.

"It was reckless and stupid," his dad continued. "And we've all done reckless, stupid things."

Surprise blossomed.

Ghost's gaze drew inward, as he looked back through his memories. His voice changed. "When your mother left us," he said quietly, "I was in a bad place. All I wanted was to be numb. The drinking, the smoking, the snorting, the fucking. If I wasn't under a table, I was on top of a groupie. Or two." Any other man would have blushed or grinned saying that. Ghost was matter-of-fact. "By the time I met Mags, I wasn't fit for anybody. I was a shit father to you. And then I knocked up a teenager."

"I'm not sure Mags was ever a teenager."

That got a small grin. "Definitely not." He shook his head. "I knew I wanted her. I had no idea she'd pull me up by the roots, shake the dirt off me, and plant me somewhere I could grow into a man again. Mags saved me," he said. "She made a home for us. She raised you. She held me accountable. I would never have become president of this club without her."

Aidan could only nod. He understood exactly the power his stepmother wielded.

Ghost sat forward, leaning toward him. "A strong leader needs a support system. He needs stability."

Oh, so that's where this was going.

"Behind every strong man is a strong woman?" he guessed.

"Beside," Ghost corrected. "She's beside him."

Because Maggie stood behind no one.

"So you're saying I need an old lady."

"Among other things. You need to get on solid ground. Maybe an old lady is the way to do that, and maybe it's not, but fucking groupies and sorority sluts isn't exactly helping your focus. A leader must be focused."

"Okay."

"Now, my uncle groomed me for this patch" – he tapped the front of his cut – "and I've let too much time go by without grooming you…"

Ghost talked for a long time, and it wasn't a lecture or an ass-chewing. Twice, he got up to get them sodas. He talked until the sternness had left him and his smiles came easier.

The shadows grew long across the floor.

Ava and Mercy both got home, but didn't come back to disturb them.

And for that time, it felt a lot like having his father back.

A lunch date with Dad. Ava had no idea what to expect. Was there some fresh danger he wanted to caution her about? Was he going to tell her that he and Maggie could no longer allow her to work at Dartmoor? Whatever it was, he'd wanted to hash it out for a while now. But Aidan's accident had thrown a wrench in everyone's everything. This asked-for lunch had been delayed, and now loomed, foreboding on the other side of the glass front door of Stella's.

Ava took a deep breath, hefted Remy's carrier higher in the crook of her arm, and entered the café.

The air conditioning was cool and soothing as it chased the humidity off her skin. Stella and Julian made a concerted effort to keep it seasonal and comfortable, never freezing the patrons. The Italian-authentic interior smelled like basil, tomatoes, and garlic. She was greeted by the usual back-and-forth calls of the kitchen staff, and the low chatter of happy customers.

Ghost had a booth by the window. He sat facing her, signaling with a two-fingered wave. Under his cut, he wore a dark green button-up with sleeves rolled to the elbows. His hair looked tame and shiny, like he'd put some sort of product in it.

Oh, Dad, she thought, biting back a smile. He was nervous. He'd tried to look nice.

Her worry ebbed.

"Hi," she said when she reached the booth.

"Hi." He stood, took the carrier from her and set it on the table. "Is he alright to sit up here?"

"Oh, yeah. That's where we put him. He's good."

Proving his point, Remy kicked his socked feet and worked his lips in and out while he stared up at his grandfather.

Ava smiled. "He says 'hi' too."

Ghost grinned at the baby, that smile he always gave Remy like he was shocked, delighted, and didn't know quite how to behave around him. The kid had him completely won over.

As they sat down across from one another, the baby commanded their attention and they were left without that normal awkwardness.

The waitress whipped by, took their drink order, and told them about the specials. Julian arrived on her heels, greeted them warmly, exclaimed over Remy. The drinks arrived; meals were ordered. And then…

They were alone.

Cue the awkward.

"So…" Ghost stirred the lemon wedge around in his tea. "How's school going?"

"It's great. Most of my professors are really engaging, and the workload's not too bad. And you know me – any time spent talking about writing is time well-spent."

His brows twitched, like he still didn't understand this passion of hers. "You've got enough time for" – he gestured toward Remy – "everything?"

"I make time for what's important, and let the little stuff shake out where it will."

He nodded. "Do you get to write your stories?"

"Not as much as I used to. But most grad students spend more time writing for class than for themselves. And a few of my school pieces will probably be submission-worthy."

Another nod and a confused frown.

Bless his heart – he could run the entire US arm of an international outlaw organization, but short stories and submissions eluded him.

It felt like it was her turn to ask something. "Merc says things are going well at Dartmoor."

"Yeah. Business is good. Things are quiet."

"That's good."

"Yeah."

"Okay," the waitress said brightly, arriving with their food.

Ava thanked her before she left them extra napkins and walked off.

More awkwardness.

"What–" they both said at the same time.

Ghost dropped his head over his spaghetti. "Go ahead."

She sighed. "Okay, I'm just going to be up-front here. I got the impression you wanted to see me for a particular reason. Is something wrong?"

He contemplated his food a moment. "Everything's fine," he said, head lifting. "So long as everything's fine with you."

She sat back, surprised. "Why wouldn't it be?"

He shrugged. Shifted in his chair. Uncomfortable. With resolute seriousness, he said, "You're happy?"

"Completely."

"You really are? School? The baby…Merc?"

"Ugh, Dad, do we have to–"

"I never really…last year, after New Orleans…I didn't get to ask you…"

"Dad–"

"I know you love him. You always have. And I know he loves you, in his own weird way. But I know the guy. I've seen him in action."

"God," she groaned, putting her face in her hands. "Please don't tell me you're asking what I think you are."

"Is he good to you? I don't mean if he pays for things and buys you a house. I mean – *is he good to you*, Ava?"

"You're asking it, aren't you?"

"I am. Yeah."

She sighed and lowered her hands to her lap, regarded her father. His cheeks were tense and dark with an embarrassed flush, but his stare was ruthless, pegging her back against the seat.

The question was so inappropriate, odd – and so touching – that she didn't know how to handle it.

"This is…sweet, in a way," she said. "But you don't really want to know details, do you?"

"No. Fuck no. But…I just want to make sure he's treating you right. I want…shit." He exhaled deeply. "I want to make sure you don't have love-goggles on, and that if there was a real problem, you'd tell your mother about it, and you wouldn't go along with him if he wasn't good to you, in every way–"

"Dad." She smiled. There was so much there: the worry, the respect, the regret. "Dad," she said again. "I don't misunderstand what Mercy is. I know how ferocious, how damaged, how violent he is. I have no delusions about that man. So it isn't just in my head that he's good to me. And he is – he is so good. He takes care of me in every way that a husband should take care of a wife."

"Yeah?"

"Yeah. And I take care of him. And we take care of Remy. And dinner." She laughed. "We're partners. Not owner and property."

He echoed her smile, though his was thin. "You're not just saying that so I won't worry?"

"Do you think I would do that?"

"No." His smile brightened a fraction. "You've got too much of your mother in you for that."

His hand lay on the table and she patted the back of it. "I turned out okay, Dad. I promise."

"I know you did, sweetheart. I know."

"We're back," Ava called as she heeled the door shut behind her. As she hefted the baby carrier through the mud room and kitchen, she was glad to hear the drone of the TV.

Aidan had ventured out into the living room.

He was sitting on the couch, watching some mindless MTV reality crap, eating a bowl of Froot Loops. He was in his now-usual uniform of baggy sweatpants and a t-shirt, but his hair was clean and shiny, and he'd shaved.

"Hey," he greeted. "Have you seen this show? It's like internet dating gone super wrong."

"Haven't seen it, don't want to see it," she said lightly, setting Remy's carrier down and dropping into the chair angled toward the sofa. "You look pretty good, bubba. How're you feeling?"

He shrugged and shoveled in Loops. "Not shitty."

"Your color's good. You've been doing your exercises?"

He rolled his eyes. "Yeah."

"You know I have to keep asking. Until you're back on your bike, I won't believe you're recovered."

No comment, just chewing.

Ava checked Remy – he was deep asleep from the car ride home – and settled back into the chair. While his eyes were fastened to the screen, she took the chance to study her brother.

He was gaining a little weight, but his appetite was still lackluster. There was an overall glassy quality about him. Dull eyes, halfhearted smiles, a general disinterest in everything.

All of that was a cover for fear.

"You know," she said, "after the crash in New Orleans, I dreaded getting back on the bike."

He darted her a look without turning his head and kept eating.

"Merc did too. You guys – you start to feel like the bike's a part of you. It's the foundation of your whole way of life. And then it becomes the thing that hurt you. It betrayed you. It's okay to feel hesitant."

"I'm not hesitant. I'm just fucked up. Physically," he clarified.

Ava gave him a small smile. "Not emotionally at all."

With an agitated huff, he sat forward and plunked his bowl down on the coffee table. "I never had a mom, and I don't need one now. Or a shrink, or whatever you're trying to be."

She kept smiling. Throughout his recovery, a casual observer would have described him as *ungrateful.* But Ava knew her brother – knew the vein of pride that ran through all the Lean Dogs – and she knew it was time for him to unpack his shame so he could let go of it.

"You know you're welcome to stay here with us as long as you need to," she said. "But I don't want you to get stuck in a place where you're too depressed and nervous to get back on track."

"I'm not depressed. And I'm sure as shit not nervous."

"No," she agreed, "and Mercy wasn't either when I couldn't get him out of bed."

He stared at her, features set in a mask of Dad-like anger.

"I'm worried about you."

"Stop."

"I can't control worry–"

"Stop being so goddamn nice to me."

"What?"

He glanced away from her, jaw grinding. He held back a second, chewing on what he wanted to say. Then he let out a deep breath. "I'm only half-related to you for godsakes," he bit out, "and you've fed me, and patched me up, and fucking bathed me, and treated me like I was your damn kid."

"And you wish I hadn't?"

"You shouldn't have had to. You gave me your fucking blood. And then you did all this…" He shook his head. "Your *blood*, Ava."

"It's your blood, too."

"Half."

"No, I don't accept that. There is no half." Her chest was tight, heart aching for him. "Aidan, I gave you the blood because it's our blood. Because I know you'd do the same for me. I'm taking care of you just like you took care of me in New Orleans. You're my brother, and there's nothing 'half' about it."

He stared at the window, tiny muscles in his face twitching.

"This isn't a favor, Aidan. Being family means there's no such thing as favors. You're my brother, and I love you, and I want you to get better."

His head turned toward her, eyes glimmering. "Dad says I need to grow up."

She inclined her head. "You do a little, yeah."

"I don't know if he's on my side, though."

"I am."

"I know." He smiled.

Fifteen
Home is a Four-Letter Word

Colin rapped on the doorjamb before he stepped into the office. Ava's mother glanced up at him as he entered.

Mercy's mother-in-law.

Mothers-in-law weren't supposed to be blonde, beautiful, and only a few years older than their sons-in-law.

Someone needed to tell that to Maggie Teague.

And maybe the same stupid ass who told her that could ask if being a child-bride ran in the family, given the obvious age advance her husband had on her.

"Oh hey," she greeted when she saw who he was. "Here for your check?"

"Yes, ma'am."

"I've got it right here." She pulled out the top desk drawer and withdrew a slip of paper.

Mercy's solution to his money problems had been straightforward. Colin had worked as an outside contractor at the Dartmoor automotive shop for the past two weeks, and in return, the boss would cut him a check and send him on his way. Much to his surprise, he hadn't hated the Lean Dogs he'd worked alongside. And though he'd stayed at the Road King, Ava had invited him for dinner often, and sent him "home" with microwavable leftovers.

Things were still...tense. But not terrible. They were...improving.

Maggie did one last survey of the check and handed it to him. Flashed him a wide, professional smile that she probably knew was gorgeous. "Here you go."

"Thanks..."

She glanced up at him with a feline sort of knowingness.

The spooky chick thing was genetic too.

"You're heading out tonight?"

"First thing in the morning."

She nodded. "Ghost wants to talk to you. He's over at the clubhouse."

Shit. What the hell did *he* want?

He pocketed the check. "Thanks."

She gave him another smile and turned back to her computer. "Have a safe trip back."

"Yeah."

He didn't trust her for a second.

Ghost was, as promised, sitting in a wrought iron chair at a café table beneath the clubhouse pavilion. Beside him, a blonde guy sat bent over a notebook, scribbling, while the president dictated.

"...and the developer? You've talked to him?"

"Not directly," the blonde said, and Colin was surprised to hear his English accent. He hadn't met Walsh yet, but he'd heard the others mention the British member. "His secretary—"

Colin cleared his throat and both of them clammed up, eyes sweeping toward him. Pale eyes and dark eyes, devoid of...everything.

Like being stared down by alpha and beta wolves. Like they were on the other side of the food chain from him.

Not creepy *at all*.

Then Ghost took a breath and his face shifted, becoming benignly polite. The socially acceptable mask sliding into place. "What's up, Colin?"

He worked hard to keep his boot soles flat on the pavement. "Maggie said you wanted to see me before I left."

Ghost nodded. "Yeah. Today your last day?"

"Yes, sir."

"She cut you a check?"

"Yes, sir."

"Good. Have a seat." He kicked out the chair beside him, the one across from Walsh.

Colin sat, because Ghost Teague came across as one of those men better off listened to.

When he was settled, the president leaned back in his chair and linked his hands over his flat stomach. "You did good work. The customers were happy with the cars you worked on. Michael and Dublin said you cleaned up after yourself in the garage." Ghost nodded. "I got no complaints." His brows lifted as if to ask, *you?*

Colin shook his head. "I appreciate the chance to work. You got a real nice operation here." Which was a massive understatement as he gestured to the entire sprawling Dartmoor complex spread out behind them.

Another nod, like the man was used to the compliments. "Merc said funds were tight at home."

Colin winced.

"You got work lined up for when you get back?"

"Nah. Figure I'll..." What? Beg Ty to take him back on at the bar? See if the chop shop behind the eighth-string voodoo boutique

155

was looking for a good fence-jumper? He'd been fired from every gig he'd ever had in New Orleans. There would be no welcome mats rolled out when he got back. "Find something," he finished lamely.

Ghost studied him a moment, dark eyes narrow. Then he glanced toward his vice president and earned a shrug in return. When he turned back, the momentary tension in his jaw had eased. "Tell you what. If you get hard up, go see Bob Boudreaux at Dog Town. He's always needing guys."

He felt his brows go up. "Dog Town. That's Lean Dogs territory down there."

"Yup, and Bob's the prez. Good guy. A good guy to have on your side." Pointed tilt of the head: *Listen well, boy.*

With a sudden *clunk*, the wheels in Colin's head started to turn. "You aren't–"

"Inviting you to prospect? Nah. That'd be Bob's decision."

His palms were suddenly damp and he spread them across his thighs. "Why would you do anything nice for me?"

Ghost shrugged. "Merc is my family. Which, by extension, makes you some kinda family."

Yeah right.

"And I ain't one to turn away potentially valuable muscle."

There was the real reason.

"Have a safe trip back," Ghost said, "and if you need to get in touch with Bob" – small, shark-like smile – "tell him I sent ya."

Ava was at her laptop when Mercy got home that evening. She held up a finger and kept typing with one hand. "Hi. Just a second. Almost…" Her lips pressed together as she concentrated on the last line and he grinned. She'd confessed that she was afraid motherhood would sap her creative energy. Instead, she'd been supercharged lately. He'd reminded her that Remy would be mobile soon, and then she'd have to chase him around. She'd decided to make the most of these first few months, computer keys clacking long into the night.

"Okay." She snapped the lid closed and shot him a smile. "Hi for real."

He stepped into the living room and leaned down to kiss her. Then turned and collapsed onto the sofa beside her. "School today?"

"Yep."

"Aidan?"

"He and Tango left about fifteen minutes ago with all his stuff. He's back at their place."

He nodded. "Good." Not that he wanted to rush the guy out of the house before he was ready...but it was time. Aidan had forever been in danger of letting the women in his life coddle him out of any authority...and perhaps he was starting to figure that out for himself.

Speaking of brothers...

"Colin's going back tomorrow," he blurted before he could catch himself.

"Mom told me." She leaned back against the cushions and turned her head toward him, expression gently probing. "You okay?"

"Uh, yeah. I want him to leave."

"Merc."

"You're getting bad as your mom, you know that?"

"You still haven't started calling him your brother."

"I don't like him."

"Doesn't change what he is."

He sighed. "Ava..."

"Fine." She threw up her hands and opened her laptop again. "I thought you might like to talk about it, but whatever." She returned to her project with a *clack-clack-clack*, skinny fingers fast at work.

He'd avoided Colin as much as possible during the weeks he'd been helping out at the auto shop. Michael had mentioned that he was a solid mechanic, but was savvy enough not to push Mercy into a conversation about him. But avoidance hadn't helped his mental obsession, because the more he dwelt on the problem, the more he realized the problem wasn't Colin at all. Colin was an asshole, but so were lots of people, and he didn't take them too seriously.

The problem was his father.

Strong, tan, gator-scarred Remy, with the wide smile and the hearty laugh and those gentle hands that had showed Mercy how to bait hooks, how to load shotguns, how to flip fried eggs so the yolks didn't break. Mercy had no bad memories of him. There was nothing but loss and grief and guilt in his heart for the man who'd raised him.

"My dad is Paul Bunyan in my head," he said.

Ava stilled, head turning toward him.

"Legendary. Larger than life. He's...he's not even human, when I think about him. He's a hero."

"He was, for raising you."

"But he was so perfect. I thought he was. And Colin..."

She sighed. "Is proof that he screwed up."

" 'Screwing up' is forgetting to stop at the store on the way home. He fucked a married woman and *had a kid*." *That he never told me about*, he added silently.

157

Ava was silent a beat, then said, "Yeah, he did. But it doesn't change how much he loved you. Or the kind of father he was to you."

"How does a good dad let his kid grow up thinking he's someone else's?" he asked on Colin's behalf.

"Well, Colin wasn't fatherless."

No. But still…

He groaned. "I dunno. I just…"

Her hand landed on his arm, stroking his biceps in slow, soothing sweeps. "It hurts."

She was right. It was that simple: it hurt like hell to come to grips with this side of his dad.

"He was supposed to be better than me," he said softly.

"Beer? Or, wait. Can you not with the prescription shit?"

Aidan shook his head as he dropped own onto the sofa. "Nah, I'm not supposed to." And funnily enough, he didn't even want one.

" 'Kay." Tango glanced around, like he was looking for some other way to help with the move-back, then sat down in the ratty La-Z-Boy across the way, the footrest popping out because weight had landed in the seat, not because the lever had been pulled. "Oh wait." He leaned forward. "You need anything? Do you want—"

"I'm good."

"You sure?"

"Yeah."

In the silence that stretched, all the apartment's ugly little sounds made themselves known: the whirring of the half-dead fridge, the clicking of the window AC unit, the unholy creaking of their upstairs neighbors shuffling around – for once it sounded like those two were walking, and not fighting or fucking.

The apartment was hideous to boot. Mashed carpet, peeling linoleum, light fixtures full of dead moths, take-out containers overflowing the kitchen trash can.

Aidan took a deep breath, regretted it thanks to the smells that assaulted him, and let it out in a rush. "Dude. We need new lives."

Holly nursed a lukewarm cup of tea at the kitchen table and listened to the garage door rattle up and then back down below her. She felt the vibration of the opener's motor through the soles of her sandals as she watched blue birds peck at the meal worms she'd left for them in a bowl outside the window. She listened to Michael's footfalls move through the basement and come up the stairs.

"Dinner smells good," he said as he entered the kitchen.

"Brisket," she said of the slab of meat in the oven that was starting to make the entire house smell like peppercorn heaven.

He walked up behind her chair, and then his hands were on her shoulders, and then he was pressing his face against the top of her head and kissing her hair. "Hi."

"Hi," she echoed, reaching to cover his hand with one of hers.

"You feeling alright?"

"Mmhm." She stroked his knuckles. "I was sitting here thinking, and I want to ask you something. Two somethings, actually."

He straightened, hands squeezing her shoulders. "Okay."

She'd been nervous about asking this a few weeks before. But the night of the ropes, they'd turned a corner into a new hallway for the two of them, one even more open and unguarded. So with a confidence that surprised her, she said, "Maggie has this tattoo. A pawprint. She said it was what Lean Dogs' old ladies got, to show they belonged." She squeezed his fingers. "You never mentioned it to me."

She swore she felt him shrug. "It doesn't matter to me. I know you're mine; no tat changes that."

Her chest swelled with bright emotion. "Really?"

"Really."

She'd thought as much, but it was nice to have it put into words.

"What was the other question?" he asked.

This was the part that had her nerves dancing. "What do you think about the name Lucy?"

"Lucy," he said, tasting the name. "Lucy McCall." She knew he was smiling when he said, "I like it."

She set her mug on the table so she could lay her hand on her belly.

Lucy.

Through the haze of smoke rising from the grill, Ava saw Colin approaching them up the back sidewalk. "He's here," she said, touching Mercy on the arm. "I'll grab drinks and be back."

He grunted an unhappy response, but his lack of verbal complaint was encouraging. At this point, Ava was convinced he only *pretended* to hate his brother.

She ducked in through the mud room door, grabbed two Buds and a tiny glass of wine for herself, then tiptoed back to the door, peering through the window at the two of them.

Colin had joined Mercy at the grill and they both stared down at the cooking burgers. Their stances were identical, the way they held themselves, the way their heads tipped forward on their necks. She could tell they were talking – the low rumble of their voices – but couldn't make out the words from her side of the door.

Then Mercy's head nodded the way it always did when he laughed. Colin mirrored the move. She heard their deep, similar chuckles.

Brothers, there was no denying it. And somehow, Ava didn't think Colin's last night in Knoxville was the end of their new connection – but the beginning.

She smiled.

~*~

There's a rhythm to everyday life within this club. Steady pulses, like heartbeats. I'm learning them, finding a way to count them. I don't know what "normal" is for other people, but this is the new normal for me, and it is wonderful. We are connected. We are family. Blood is measured by halves – and we are stronger for it.

Holly McCall

THE END

Half My Blood

Lauren Gilley is the author of thirteen novels and several short stories. She lives in the South, obsessing about the lives of imaginary people.

Get Connected:

Blog: hoofprintpress.blogspot.com

Facebook: Lauren Gilley – Author

Twitter: @lauren_gilley

Instagram: hppress

Email: authorlaurengilley@gmail.com

Half My Blood

Other Titles From Lauren Gilley

The Walker Series
Keep You
Dream of You
Better Than You
Fix You
Rosewood

Whatever Remains

Shelter

The Russells
Made for Breaking
God Love Her
Keeping Bad Company
"Things That Go Bang in the Night"
"Green Like the Water"

Dartmoor Series
Fearless
Price of Angels
Half My Blood
The Skeleton King

Made in the USA
Coppell, TX
22 August 2020